DAUGHTER

Ana María Shua

English translation by Andrea G. Labinger

literalpublishing

First edition, 2020
© Ana María Shua
© 2019 Literal Publishing
5425 Renwick Dr.
Houston , TX 77081
www.literalmagazine.com

ISBN: 978-1-942307-34-1

*Printed & Bounced by The Country Press, Inc. P. O. Box 489
Middleborough, MA 02346-0489*

Table Of Contents

This novel includes the diary of its construction, unnecessary but perhaps interesting.

It is printed in a different font so that readers may comfortably exercise their right to ignore it.

On the Ship

The ship was as huge as death. From the dock, from nearby, from down below, its most impressive aspect was the enormous height of the hull. Esmé hugged her parents again, wishing they would leave once and for all so that she could begin exploring and cut short the whole farewell business. Guido was fascinated by the cabin. The carefully considered perfection of the tiny, essential furniture, the fold-up bunk beds, the bathroom door that turned into a closet door, the fittings. They would really have liked a porthole, but the stateroom was below the water line.

Ramiro, the other copywriter from the advertising agency where Esmé worked, arrived out of breath, his curls flying. He had somehow managed to wangle permission to board the ship, and he was brandishing a check in his hand.

"I got that bastard Beláustegui to pay us for the free-lance job."

"What a son-of-a-bitch, sending my check to the ship," Esmé said. "But I'll cash it anyway."

She endorsed the check and handed it to her father, now feeling extremely grateful that he was there.

Many people were leaving for real, leaving-leaving. You could tell by the amount of luggage. Guido and Esmé weren't sure yet. They could always come back if they wanted to. There were some familiar faces. A schoolmate of Esmé's, sitting on top of a pile of bundles that he'd no doubt have to store in the hold. A lawyer Guido knew. The ocean liner, accustomed to crossing the sea with a cargo of men and women of a certain age, people with plenty of time and money to discover Europe or rediscover it, as well as immigrants who wanted to reverse the journey they'd made back in the days when they had more illusions than cash, now carried many young couples in its metal belly, some of them with babies or little children who scurried around between the ropes, excited, frightened, heedless of their parents' shouts.

"They all have kids," Esmé's mother remarked to Esmé, who understood her and also hated her a little.

"Esmeralda," her father said, with a final embrace. Only when he was very angry or very emotional did her father call her by her full name.

On her second day at sea, Esmé was still dizzy from the motion of the ship, but not as much as she had feared. The sheer size of the beast made the rolling less noticeable. On the other hand, being trapped in the unrelieved immensity of the ocean gave her a feeling of claustrophobia.

There were three decks, each with its own swimming pool, dining room, and recreation areas. Esmé and Guido tried to sneak a peek at the first class rooms, but strict controls prohibited the different classes from mixing. At least not upwardly. However, they had no problem visiting the third class accommodations, which didn't strike them as too different from tourist. As usual, the rich had the right to poke their noses into the staterooms of the poor, but not the other way around, though no one on the ocean liner was really poor. Of course, in tourist class, everyone remarked on how much fun they were having compared to those in first class, with their ridiculous formal dress requirement for meals. There was a movie theater, a real movie theater with a large screen and more than a hundred seats. There was skeet shooting (*tiro al piatello*) every morning, but they never got up early enough to take part. In one area accessible to all classes, there was a shopping gallery that at first seemed enormous and well-stocked, almost like an actual street where you could buy French designer clothing, Italian shoes and purses, Swiss chocolates and watches, silk scarves, and pay for them in dollars or Italian lire. But after browsing a couple of times, Guido and Esmé realized that it was really a small-scale model of a street, and there were only four or five shops. Guido, who had never been a militant, was nonetheless a strict theoretical Marxist, as ardent as the best of them, and he had little patience for luxuries: there was no need to succumb; it was important to keep a critical distance.

Most importantly, there were meals. Italian, abundant, varied. Theme dinners. One day the second class dining room (referred to as "tourist class") was decorated to resemble a Spanish inn, and on another day, it was festooned with nets and fishing poles to become a dockside restaurant. Decked out in berets and striped tee shirts, with sashes around their waists, kerchiefs adorning their necks, or in sequin-embroidered vests, the waiters dressed up successively as *gondolieri*, French Apaches, or bullfighters. There was a cold appetizer, generally a mixed antipasto, the requisite pasta course, always delicious and *al dente*, a main course, a cheese plate, fruit, and dessert. Fresh-baked bread was served with breakfast every morning. In the afternoon they brought out tea with cakes and puddings, which, after a lunch like that, very few travelers were in any condition to enjoy. Mealtimes were announced with a lively, catchy tune that by the second day had already begun to activate people's salivary glands.

Every morning an announcement of the latest cable news was distributed throughout the cabins. On the second day, one of the cables reported that along La Costanera in Buenos Aires twenty dynamited bodies had been found. Approximately twenty. As it was impossible to identify the remains, the news cable said, they had been designated "N.N.", or "no name."

And it was all so much fun! Thirteen days to Lisbon. Guido's lawyer acquaintance, who was approaching fifty, was traveling with Mausi, a psychologist who, by sheer coincidence, happened to be Esmé's distant relative. They were going to Barcelona, with plans to settle in Sitges. The Catalonian town had become a Mecca for Argentines.

They had lunch and dinner together every day. Mausi was a tall, slender woman with very short hair and a charming elegance that informed all her gestures. Among members of Esmé's family, she was considered scandalous. When Mausi divorced for the first time, she left her children with her husband, a shocking, inconceivable decision. How could any mother want or be able to free herself of her children? She couldn't, she wouldn't: not a real mother. The lawyer with whom she was traveling to Europe was her third partner. Esmé had heard other women in the family speak of her with a mixture of horror, admiration, rejection, and envy.

Mausi seemed so imbued with her feminist ideas that it was hard not to tease her a little. Esmé pretended to be a shy, submissive young woman who followed Guido's orders to the letter. Mausi prodded her into rebelling with long, enlightening speeches that the young couple rehashed in their cabin, convulsed with laughter.

One of Mausi's children had been killed a few months earlier in an alleged attempt to flee as he was being transferred from the Sierra Chica prison. Another, a daughter from her first marriage, had escaped in time and lived in Mexico. Feeling threatened by the authorities, Mausi had decided to go to Spain with Edgardo, leaving a five-year-old girl with her second husband. (What kind of mother?). Edgardo had also been threatened, for defending a union leader.

With so many young people around, the atmosphere aboard the ship was very animated. Nearly every night there were parties and dances. A live band played the same popular classics over and over, which they interpreted wearily and indifferently while the passengers danced with enthusiasm. There was also a series of pre-established rituals, which were nothing new for the crew, but which the passengers were experiencing for the first – and probably only – time in their lives. The Crossing-the-Equator ritual took place at noon. Many passengers wore disguises. Esmé pretended she wanted to participate, Guido pretended to forbid it, and so they provoked one of Mausi's best feminist arguments. Her partner, however, began to suspect.

The Crossing-the-Equator ritual consisted of tossing female passengers, vaguely dressed as Polynesians (fake grass mini-skirts; crepe-paper leis), into the swimming pool. They cooperated gladly, laughing and screaming. Naturally, one of the first to fall into the water was Mónica Sternberg. Esmé knew her because she had gone to camp with Mónica's two brothers. Alejo Sternberg, the younger one, had dropped out of his program in Economics and was now working as a dishwasher in Málaga. Mónica was gorgeous. Every morning a group of men, including Guido, would form a ring on the second-class (tourist) deck to watch her from above as she played ping-pong in her bikini on the third-class deck.

The older brother, Guillermo, had been abducted from his house one night. People said that he, like many others, was locked up in a property belonging to the Navy. People said he had been tortured, that he was still alive. It was strange to pass certain places in Buenos Aires, certain buildings, walking or in a car, and to know that friends or relatives or acquaintances were locked in there, kidnapped, tortured, but alive. Esmé envied Mónica's waist and her green eyes, and she also envied the anguish of her knowing that her brother had disappeared, instead of the firm certainty of her own sister's bullet-riddled corpse, which they had picked up at the court morgue. In a few years, no doubt, those who had gone missing would be legalized and judged, or possibly freed outright.

On the ocean liner everything was carefully calculated for the passengers' pleasure, including the erotic adventures of female passengers with members of the crew. The officers on board seemed to have been chosen for their attractiveness. They were all tall, with smart haircuts and an impeccable appearance. To Esmé they seemed a little unreal, with their pristine white shirts and their bright smiles always at the ready. They spoke in a charming Italian or a sing-song Spanish that the women loved to hear whispered in their ears. The captain seemed impregnable, but it was rumored that the first mate had fallen victim to Mónica Sternberg's relentless barrage. There were relatively few officers, and thus it wasn't easy for them to attend to so many eager female passengers properly, but they multiplied and worked miracles. Or so people said.

Esmé had nightmares. One night she dreamed of seeing bloody corpses slipping through a porthole. A rain of dead people that plunged into the depths at an impossible speed, like human cannonballs, as though they were being shot from a cannon on high, aimed at the ocean floor. Guidó heard her screaming and clambered down from his bunk to shake her. When she awoke, the nightmare was still there.

Sooner or later, for enjoyment or entertainment's sake, people need to compete, or at least watch others do so. Of course that very human need had been adequately foreseen. In addition to the famous skeet-shooting, which every evening Esmé and Guido vowed to watch and every morning forgot about, there were all sorts of contests. Dance contests, costume competitions, talent shows, *truco* tournaments, canasta, backgammon, and Scrabble competitions, but no poker. Esmé studied the players' faces, trying to guess which ones were tourists, *real* tourists, which were the ones who would return to the country after a few weeks of fun in Europe. Sometimes she thought she couldn't identify anyone. In the costume competitions, the prize for most original costume went to a bright-eyed young man dressed as a folding chair. That was the classmate she had recognized at the dock with his wife and baby.

She didn't have to ask *him* anything. Her high school classmates were falling like flies, like ants, like cockroaches, but with less ability to survive. When she was a girl, at Carnival time, her father had dressed her and her sister as accident victims. With carefully assembled, ketchup-stained bandages, their arms in slings and limping, they would join the throngs in the streets before the pitying gazes of the ladies, who, taken aback, would ask what had happened to the poor little things. Now the idea of dressing up as an accident victim no longer appealed to her, and, as with many childhood diversions, she found it hard to recall why it had seemed so funny at the time.

Esmé spent long hours reading on deck, lying in a *chaise longue*, her legs covered with a blanket, even though it was warm. It was a somewhat uncomfortable position, glamorized by literature and film. She and Guido shared a passion for film: the little theater on the ocean liner, always full, fascinated and seduced them. They went every day, even seeing children's movies. The ship's program carefully avoided dramas and was restricted to comedies and action films. It might not have been their first choice, but even that was pleasant for them, not having to choose. Esmé tried to avoid looking at the daily schedule so that it would be a complete surprise. She sat down and watched the screen with the illusions of a little girl.

In one very violent film, two policemen from California abandoned all attempts to stay within the law in order to fight evil with the weapons of evil. It was a story with a moral, justifying the inevitable consequences of acting outside the law to defend the law, a little like *Dirty Harry*, which Clint Eastwood had popularized a few years before and which would have been unthinkable for the previous generation, where, at least in films, the heroes were always impeccably legal, fair, and good. In one sequence where the detectives kicked in an apartment door and burst in firing a machine gun, Esmé felt sick to her stomach, no doubt due to the ship's rocking, and they had to leave the theater. A strong wind had come up, and they were entering the Bay of Biscay, where the sea is always rough. Guido made her take a Dramamine, and she lay down in the bunk bed till dinnertime.

The ship docked in Lisbon. Not too long before, the dictatorship of Caetano, Salazar's successor, had fallen, and for the first time in 48 years, the Portuguese had voted in free elections. What struck Esmé and Guido most were the walls painted with political slogans, giving the city a dirty, careless aspect. They went to the Botanical Gardens, arriving back at the ship just in time. Nearly everyone disembarked in Spain. In the port of Barcelona the *Eugenio C* deposited its cargo of frightened, young, excited Argentines, happy to be alive, glad to have arrived, to have run away, mutilated. Youth is happiness.

JOURNAL ENTRY 1

I'm reading a book Lucía gave me. She knows how to pick them. It's called (a bold title) *HhHH*. The author is a French writer, Laurent Binet. It's about the attack on Heidrich, head of the Gestapo, Prague, 1943. Rigorously historical. And yet.

And yet it's something more, or it's something else. Because simultaneously, along with the rendering of historical facts or the description of documents, Binet keeps a journal of his own investigation, in which he doesn't skimp on sensations, failures, feelings.

I wonder if it would be possible to achieve something similar with a work of fiction. Fiction is constructed like dreams. You don't dream of things you don't know; the dream reorganizes the materials you're familiar with when awake.

What is created: nothing, practically nothing. A construction based on the same old materials, derived from structures predetermined by tradition. Just like the Spaniards in the New World, who destroyed a pagan temple in order to use the blocks to build a church.

What is created: maybe just some slight, new interconnection between the parts, a subtle departure from certain norms whose application must be controlled.

Like in dreams: nothing more than a different combination of factors, that nonetheless alters, alters, alters the result.

Would it be possible then, to write a novel that documents the process of its own construction? A collection of data but also the novelist's problems and difficulties? Partially. It wouldn't be the first time, of course. In an historical reconstruction like Binet's, the die is cast. Even though they may not know the details, readers know the outcome ahead of time. This allows the author to make unconstrained remarks about what will happen next, without fear of ruining the suspense, which is maintained (perfectly) by other tools. In a purely fictional work, on the other hand, it's not possible or advisable to reveal beforehand what the author plans to do with her characters. It's impossible to mention the difficulties encountered in trying to stick to the path because the idea is to hide the final outcome (which, besides, can change, even for the author, as the writing progresses) from the reader. But it *is* possible to describe how the collection of materials was developed and perhaps even certain general directions in which the discourse will advance.

The journal of the novel will always pretend to be documentary, but it will also contain a large dose of fiction. We shall see.

Paris Was a Party, and We Weren't Invited

What her mother said was true. They all had kids, and that didn't make their life easier, Esmé thought, once again justifying her decision to postpone them. In Barcelona they met up with the Lúquezes, who had arrived from Peru and were living with their two children in the little room of a *pensión* that provided them with lunch, but not dinner. The children were pouncing on some long, greenish pears with brown spots that Guido and Esmé had brought from the ship, and they gnawed on them without comment, with very little joy. But Ana Lúquez had already founded a job at a Catalonian advertising agency and was waiting for her first paycheck to move out, to have dinner.

That night they took the Talgo to Paris. They traveled in a shared compartment car, rocked by the motion of the train. They slept because they were young. They were going to Paris because they were Argentine, because they were Latin American, because they had read Cortázar, because they thought Paris was the be-all and the end-all, the zenith and the nadir, the microcosm of the universe, madness, wonder, Gog and Magog, the place of freedom, of creation, the navel of the world, and, especially, of *la vie bohème*, the city where art strolled naked through the streets. They were going to Paris because Paris was Paris and it had struggled mightily, for eons, with the task of creating that fantastic illusion of Paris in the world.

It had never occurred to them to consider what Paris thought of them.

Paris wasn't waiting for them, didn't want them, didn't love them.

Paris was a hard city, one that wasn't interested in poor immigrants. The City of Light was also the Gray City. Barcelona had seemed gray to them because of the condition of its streets and its buildings, because of its inhabitants' threadbare clothing, their tired and humble demeanor. In Paris the sun came out occasionally, in summer and part of spring. In Paris it drizzled. Always. The famous Parisian drizzle was beautiful and literary for an entire week. But then it went on. Esmé woke up in the morning, flung open the shutters in the studio apartment, and once again found herself facing a ceiling of clouds that swept away her desire to live.

Besides, they would need to earn some money in order to live. To earn some money, it wouldn't have been a bad idea to have her papers in order, some sort of legal status. Esmé and Guido had entered the country on tourist visas.

They lived on the sixth floor of a building without an elevator, with such a small bathroom that they had to shower while sitting on the toilet. It was a *studio*, a nice, prestigious title when seen from the other side of the ocean (*Dear Lili: We're in Paris and we're renting a cute studio …*), but which in Paris served to define, in the most prosaic way, a tiny, one-room apartment. They rented it furnished. Since the box spring that served as their mattress was worn out, they turned it upside down and squeezed it between the legs of the bed. They covered themselves with stained, tightly woven, light, but warm, blankets, army castoffs they had bought at the Flea Market. To keep warm, they spread out over the blankets the very symbol of their Argentine-ness, their *gamulanes*, those suede, sheepskin jackets, heavy and useful on freezing nights. They ate for three francs at the university restaurant. As evening fell, they peered anxiously and penniless into the windows of the *charcuteries*. At the bakery they bought baguettes; at the supermarket they bought butter and pork liver paté, which was quite delicious, you had to admit (they exchanged another complicit glance). It was *French food*.

Paris distilled nectar to attract the bees that repaid her with their honey. But in the process she couldn't avoid collecting flies. Even the flies, when seen from outside, and thanks to the city's prestige and subtle intelligence, formed part of her crown. But from within, what you had to do was fight them off with insecticide and flyswatters. Esmé and Guido were flies. They suddenly realized that, in fact, the characters in *Hopscotch* had never been happy in Paris, no matter how much happiness Cortázar, with the magic of his prose, brought to his readers.

To have a full bathroom and kitchen, even without a tub, was a privilege shared by few of their friends. Some had a bathroom but no kitchen. There were others who shared a bath down the hall with neighbors on their floor. Many lived in *chambres de bonnes*, those tiny, airless rooms on the top floor, with no bathroom and sometimes so diminutive that the bed was wedged between two walls.

They worked. They exhausted all the sad jobs of the undocumented. Every three months they crossed the border and returned in order to renew their tourist residency permits. Esmé found a temporary waitressing job at a Spanish food expo, but she lost it as soon as she dropped her first tray: wine, glasses, and all.

The two of them distributed flyers; he helped unload trucks; she took on cleaning jobs. Esmé tried to offer Spanish classes but only managed to find an exchange for French lessons. Guido thought he might get hired on for the grape harvest, but he had arrived too late.

The mailman came by three times a day. Esmé anxiously rooted around in the mailbox, looking for those light blue-and-white bordered envelopes, ripped open and glued back together by a censorship that didn't bother to conceal itself, but rather, quite the contrary, modestly participated in the consolidation of terror, those envelopes filled with thin, ultra-fine paper, airmail paper, full of insinuated news, banal words that hid the stories no one dared write. And if her sister Regina's presence overflowed her dreams, her absence squeezed Esmé's arteries, took her breath away each time she stuck her hand in the mailbox, believing, against all rationality, against all memory, believing without knowing what, out of oblivion itself, that one of the envelopes would bear her name written in her dead sister's small, uneven hand.

They both had nightmares. Guido's were confused, and he couldn't or wouldn't talk about them. He would get up in the middle of the night to splash his face with cold water. Esmé often dreamed of her *compañeros*, the youngest ones, those she had been in charge of, especially those she had seduced and abandoned, those she had persuaded to join the militants. As she didn't know their real names or addresses, nor did she have any way to communicate with them or with anyone who knew them, she had no idea what had become of them. Their faces came back to her in dreams time and again, and while her sister returned, too, alive, intact, and demanding, perhaps as punishment, perhaps because that made it even more painful to awaken once more to her absence, the others, though they might be talking and moving about in her dreams, always returned dead.

If she had a daughter, Esmé would name her after her sister. She wanted to have a daughter in order to give her her sister's name. It was necessary, urgent, and constant to remind herself that she didn't want to have children yet. But if she did. If she ever did.

They got together with lots of fellow Argentines and other Latin Americans, all of them young, nearly all exiles, some with children who had been born in France but who were refused French citizenship by the laws of descendancy and denied Argentine citizenship by the laws of residency. During the dictatorship, the Argentine Embassy was ordered not to accept citizenship applications for babies who had been born in Europe during those years, so the little ones had the legal status of pariahs, stateless babies whose mothers nursed them guiltily, anxiously, proudly.

Perhaps because the reality of being in Paris somehow pushed them toward the diffuse borders of art, and also because Guido hadn't found a way or a place to channel his vocation and his unfinished, useless law studies, impossible to complete in a country with a different language and different laws; perhaps because they filled their many empty days between one temp job and another by going to the movies, where they'd often stay and watch the same film over and over, or visiting museums, the infinite museums of Paris; perhaps because of their friendship with the son of Vitale, an Argentine painter who lived in France, Guido began to talk about one of his long-lost desires – buried for a time beneath the mountain of obligations incumbent upon a student of law and Marxism. As a non-militant but strict Marxist, Guido had participated in dozens of study groups, had read Marx and Engels in the original, without, however, belittling their disseminators, like Marta Harnecker, author of that generational bible known as *Basic Concepts of Historical Materialism.* He had read Gramsci and Rosa Luxemburg and Paulo Freire; he had read the anarchists – Bakunin, Kropotkin – so as to be able to discuss them; he had read Trotsky and Lenin and knew the *Communist Manifesto* literally by heart. But now, in Paris, he wanted to paint.

Esmé was caught off-guard. She hadn't been aware of this new fact of her husband's character and didn't know if she approved. Guido became a habitué of Vitale's studio, where he met with the painter's old and young friends to discuss the tendencies and styles of European art, especially defending old-style, prestigious easel painting and attacking the facile nonsense that was conceptual art.

"Art isn't made of ideas. Ideas are for people like you," he told Esmé in a dismissive tone, "for you advertising types. Art is realization. Art is every brushstroke."

Little by little he became impregnated with the corresponding technical vocabulary and began saving everything he could in order to buy an easel, canvases, stretchers, oil paints, brushes.

"Sable," he said in a reverent voice when Esmé was scandalized at the price of a paintbrush.

The one-room apartment they lived in was small, very small, and when it started to fill up with canvases, dirty paint rags, containers of pigment, white plaster models or colored wax ones, when Guido brought in the door-table on which he mixed his colors, experimented with very expensive oils (Rembrandt or Windsor and Newton brands), relegating Esmé's typewriter to a corner, the situation became desperate. The smell, more than anything else, exasperated Esmé whenever she came in from the street and felt her hair, her clothing, her skin, saturated with that fug of oil paint, linseed, and turpentine that seemed to make Guido happy in a way that was hard to communicate, which he demonstrated by taking deep breaths while he donned his painting gear – a old, stained sweater and a pair of pants.

The strangest thing was that Guido didn't paint.

Guido turned up his nose at preliminary sketches, was against acrylics, which he considered simplistic, and worked in the old-fashioned way with linen canvases, which he refused to buy pre-stretched and mounted; he mixed his own pigments in order to achieve a unique palette, a palette of his own, *his* palette, which would differentiate him from all the other painters in this world. He used a door mounted on easels, a big, broken-down door that someone had tossed out in the street to be carried off with the trash and which Guido had managed to shove into the studio with help and great difficulty. There were cans where he sorted his brushes (thick and fine, square and round), by shape. And on the walls there was a proliferation of spatulas. Guido considered himself part of the *neo-figurative* movement, which repudiated exhibits and happenings in favor of traditional painting. He made sketches in notepads with special paper, and he even managed to slap a few daubs of paint on the canvases. But he never finished any of his paintings.

At that time Esmé had found a job as an *au pair* and was taking care of a blonde little three-year-old boy, the son of a couple of Swedes. All he was interested in was building towers of blocks, and he wasn't at all happy about his caregiver's attempts to smother him in the South American hugs or kisses that his parents seemed to disapprove of wordlessly, with their looks, with their behavior, as if Esmé had been trying to smear the boy's cheeks – always so clean, so white, so golden – with a thick layer of saliva contaminated with third-world bacteria.

"What if you tried to give painting classes? We could put up signs …"

"No. I've already told you I don't want to give classes. And I don't want to do crafts, either. I don't want to do anything that would be a cartoon. I'd rather carry bags down at the docks than bastardize Art."

Guido always said "Art" with a capital A, never bastardized it, and didn't carry bags down at the docks, either. On the other hand, he had discovered a small enterprise that could finance his outrageously expensive passion: smuggling used cars over from Holland and selling them in Paris. In Holland cars quickly depreciated in value, among other reasons because the older the car, the more expensive the license plate became. After four or five years, the Dutch got rid of their cars for ridiculous prices. It was essential to cross the border without causing suspicion, and then, with a simple ad on the windshield, the vehicle would sell for a good profit in Paris.

But most importantly, Guido had joined (with the same dose of fanaticism he had devoted in his own country to discussions of Marxism) the myriad of Latin American Artists in Paris who fought for the purity of Art without practicing it. He now belonged to the legion of painters who didn't paint, writers who didn't write, composers who didn't make music, sculptors who didn't sculpt, actors who didn't act, but who nonetheless got together, argued, drank (preferably absinthe), and especially, *lived* in Paris, an activity that appeared to validate their pretensions, which in a way excused them from practicing their art.

One morning Esmé opened the blinds, expecting the sun, which didn't appear, and then went downstairs, as usual, to buy *croissants* for breakfast (six *croissants ordinaries*, as the French, perhaps unfairly, called what for Argentines were *medialunas de grasa*). It was raining. A letter from Buenos Aires said that Lucio and Guillermo weren't there. Esmé read the sentence many times, as if she might discover new meaning in the arabesques of the letters. They were two brothers who had been dating her cousins. Lucio, the older one, was well-groomed, blond. Guillermo was eighteen years old and had very curly hair. Now they weren't there: they weren't there. She considered phoning, but she was afraid.

Shortly before Esmé and Guido left Buenos Aires, Guillermo and her cousin Dorita had asked permission to sleep at their house. They were tired, dirty, and grumpy. For the last week they had spent their nights coming and going by bus: that's what it meant to go *underground*. Esmé and Guido's apartment was dangerous, too. They stayed just one night.

That afternoon, in Paris, Esmé plucked up her courage and went to the post office to make a phone call.

"I got your letter. Guillermo and Lucio aren't there? Not there at all?" she ventured to ask.

"No," replied her aunt in the same, energetic voice as always.

"But what does it mean, they aren't there?"

"It means exactly what you think. It means they're not here anymore, for twenty days now. Don't worry about your cousins; we shipped them off to Spain."

Esmé held out the hope that Lucio and Guillermo were alive. She kept hanging on to that hope for a few more years.

JOURNAL ENTRY 2

The imperfection of the imperfect tense when it comes time to narrate. I'm writing the second chapter, perhaps too long, in the pathetic imperfect tense: they used to go out, they used to eat, they would jump, they would think, they often felt. The imperfect isn't a narrative tense. It's useful for describing how things were, but it's useless for telling what happened. Strangely, this was a problem I had in my very first attempts at narration, when I was trying to shift from poetry to the short story. For some reason, I was easily able to describe what everything was like, but I failed when it was time to tell *what happened next*. It didn't feel natural to me; I had to force myself, use phony language, in order to be able to break the web of the situation, to burst into the story. *Then, suddenly, once,* miraculous words that call for the preterit. *Suddenly, one day* breaks into the action, the magic is produced: I found myself narrating. But there was nothing magical about it. It was slow, deliberate, and forced.

Something similar is happening to me now. For some reason I feel the need to keep telling what was happening before I get to what happened. Maybe because I'm trying to create a life story, a story that should develop over the course of many years. What are they doing? What are the others doing?

I'm reading a book by Herta Müller, *The Hunger Angel*. It's a novel about a forced labor camp in Russia, after the war, where hundreds of young, German-speaking Romanians are imprisoned. In other books (*The Passport*), in order to tell the harshest, most brutal tales, Herta Müller deploys a gorgeous, poetic prose – complex, difficult, and enormously pleasant. This book, which doesn't lack for poetry, is, on the other hand, written in a simple, direct way. I've read about two hundred pages of imperfect tense with very brief action scenes that almost serve to illustrate the descriptions. So it's possible.

Information: C. and R. told me at great length about the smuggling – or near smuggling – of Dutch cars in the seventies. C. transported them to Madrid on behalf of someone else, while R. personally "imported" minivans to Paris. The information they gave me was fascinating and much more than I needed for this novel. When it came time to use it, I realized that if I continued in that direction, I was going to lose track of my objective. Regardless, I'm glad I asked them: even if only two sentences show up on a topic, they should be coherent and error-free.

I interview my friend X, a visual artist, to get information about Guido's activities in Paris. X was a political refugee in Europe. We meet at La Biela, a café popular among young people in the seventies. But not with hippies or militants or intellectuals. We preferred the cafés on Corrientes: El Colombiano, Ramos, La Paz, Politeama, El Foro, La Giralda. Only those people we called "bananas" went to the cafés on Libertador or to La Biela, which has proven to have a ridiculously loyal clientele. It's them, the same ones, the kids who showed up on their motorcycles in the sixties and seventies and now are in their sixties and seventies themselves. Without motorcycles.

X didn't live in Paris in those days. However, he explains to me in great detail what articles Guido might have kept in his studio. Which brushes, what kind of canvases, what colors; he even knows at which store in Paris you could buy them.

Today the world has discovered Buenos Aires and launches constant hordes of tourists into the city. La Biela is in an excellent tourist district. Behind us, a couple skillfully dances the tango and the milonga. The sound of the recording is pretty annoying, but it's a lovely day and we'd rather be outdoors. X describes the material objects to me very precisely, but he's less good at recalling the sort of discussions that might have taken place in that artistic milieu. I prod him. Which artists were iconic, which were controversial? Le Parc? Warhol? Minujín? What were the Themes? He talks a lot about installations, but I have my doubts. Did they even use that word in the seventies? I think I heard it for the first time around fifteen or twenty years ago. But maybe they really did use it then in the visual arts world. And in the world of socially committed art. Sure, he's right. *That* I do remember intensely. The very recent (in the seventies) kingdom of posters, the art of social protest, collective art, art by and for everyone. Ah, memory! That fake landscape, a disgusting stage set infested with doubts and lies.

The Ambassador

As the years passed, slowly in their unfolding, devastatingly swiftly when viewed in retrospect, the exiles' situation started to improve. Guido and Esmé obtained legal residency, the Dutch used car business prospered, and they were able to move to another apartment on the second floor, a little bigger, with no kitchen, but with a bathroom that was big enough to include the presence of that symbol of luxury, a bathtub. Esmé's sense of relief on moving soon disappeared when Guido once again set up his easels, his oils, his solvents, and his get-togethers with friends, those Latin American painters who, with the occasional exception, painted as little as he did but, who, on the other hand, smoked dark tobacco cigarettes, Gauloises or Gitanes, creating ephemeral art in the form of puffs of smoke that disappeared in the air almost as quickly as the sound of their words.

Among them was Biltz, a boy who insisted on wearing the bushy, Beatles-style sideburns that were already beginning to look outdated. Perhaps because of his eternal good humor and his personal affability, perhaps because he spoke French well – and English, too – Biltz had found himself one of the best jobs in the exile milieu, even at a time when many were just starting to get a handle on the language, obtain their papers, and were on the road to legal residency. Biltz was a chauffeur for the ambassador of a Central American republic, whom he described as an enormous, generous man who, despite his position, could barely speak French. Thanks to Biltz and his personal charm, Esmé found work as a babysitter/instructor for the twins.

These were the daughters of the self-same ambassador, five years old, bright-eyed and fun, with light brown hair and skin the color of milky tea. The father was a serious-looking man who hardly spoke to Esmé. Just as Biltz had described him, he was large, and – in some ways – also generous: he paid her well. When he took her into his service, following a long conversation in which he inquired about her knowledge and education, he handed her a paper with written instructions that included details about the complex relationship with the other staff members: the cook, the two cleaning women, his wife's chauffeur and his own, the dining room butler, and especially the *real* babysitter, a Portuguese girl who was in charge of caring for the twins, dressing and feeding them, and who seemed to be quite jealous of the relationship between the little ones and Esmé.

With regard to the Ambassador, Esmé felt a combination of fear and rejection, no doubt caused by his implacable, stiff politeness, a frozen block of courtesy that was impossible to penetrate. He had been brought up at English boarding schools and had studied political science at Oxford. He played classical music with unexpected sensitivity on the huge piano in the main living room.

His wife was a Peruvian woman, so white that she seemed to be coated in limestone. She belonged to a down-at-the-heels family from the local aristocracy. When they met, he was a bureaucrat at his country's embassy in Peru, and she didn't mind confessing how awestruck she had been with his economic power, the promise of a life filled with cocktail parties and formal dinners, with a different dress for every occasion, luxury cars, and plenty of jewelry. She was a frivolous, lively, affectionate girl; her daughters adored her and ran to embrace her when she returned home in the afternoon, laden with packages from the shopping expeditions that seemed to make her as happy as she had imagined when she agreed to marry her husband.

In this case, the Latin American hugs were viewed favorably, and Esmé never had the feeling that the twins would need to go through a disinfection process as soon as their babysitter went home.

If the mother's homecoming caused the girls to burst with joy, their father's arrival introduced a somber note. They lived in a beautiful old building on Rue Marigny, in an enormous apartment that could easily hold twenty studios like Guido and Esmé's. All the rooms were immense, and a gust of icy air seemed to pass through all of them whenever the twins' father opened the front door.

Esmé's job consisted of entertaining them for a few hours when they came home from kindergarten. She had been chosen for this task because of her good French, because she was a Spanish speaker, and because of her cultural level in general. She played with them, read them stories in French and in Spanish, played music previously selected by their father. Raised in an atmosphere of rigid customs, which not even their mother dared defy, the girls were very well-behaved and only rarely disobeyed an order or acted silly.

One afternoon Esmé was reading aloud in the twins' room, absorbed in the adventures of Babar the Elephant, without realizing that only María Lourdes was listening to her, while Cecilia, the more mischievous of the two, had left the room without making a sound. The extreme calm and silence alerted Esmé, who put the book aside and went out to look for the little girl, followed by María Lourdes. She found Cecilia in the piano room, captivated by a forbidden activity: she had taken off her shoes and was running around in stocking feet, pretending to skate on the waxed floor. They didn't know that the Ambassador was at home. When the child realized that her father was watching her, her fright made her lose her balance and fall to the floor.

Just as if he hadn't seen her, the father walked in and sat down on the piano bench. Esmé tried to take the girls away, but they remained there, each in her place, like frozen statues. They knew what was about to come and they also knew that trying to escape would have been worse.

Utterly calm, the father called Cecilia over. The child got up and walked slowly toward the piano, dragging her feet, which seemed to resist the signals given by her brain. When she was right next to him, the father ordered her to turn around and squat. Composed, without the slightest nervous response, and without anger, like someone imparting a fair and necessary punishment, and looking for a place on her body where he wouldn't harm her, the father smacked her on the behind hard enough to send her flying forward, and she almost (but just *almost*; the calculation was precise) hit her head against the wall. Cecilia fell again, this time biting her lower lip. Esmé expected to hear her burst into sobs, but the child knew how to respond better than her sitter did. She stood up and wiped her mouth with the back of her hand in complete silence, while tears ran down her dark cheeks. The ambassador was already playing the first chords of a piano composition by Debussy.

"Wash her face, Esmeralda," he ordered. "And don't let them back into this room."

Esmé realized that she couldn't and wouldn't keep working in that house. And she also realized, for the first time, something that not even the easy affection she had for the twins had awakened in her body. She realized that she wanted to have a child whom she would never hit and never allow anyone else to hit. It was then that Esmé began to feel that almost physical sensation beginning to grow within her, a feeling she secretly called "the urge for a child."

JOURNAL ENTRY 3

My friend L. lived in Paris for fifteen years. I knew that at some point she had worked as a babysitter for the daughters of an African ambassador. That experience might have awakened the desire for a child in my character. I began writing the chapter without talking to L. My imaginary ambassador was married to a compatriot, as black as he was, and the entire household staff was black, as well. I wanted my friend to tell me about her real experience, but L. is very reserved. She doesn't speak much about her life in Paris, and I was afraid to bother her with my questions. In fact, I hate interrogating people, even though life has taught me that no invented story is as fascinating and unconventional as reality.

At last we got together at a café famous for the variety and quality of its pastries. It was 2012, and although the word *confitería* was no longer being used in Buenos Aires, it might have described the place more precisely. With each cup of coffee they brought us a tiny and delicious sample of the house's confectionary skills. As the chocolate mousse melted in our mouths, I discovered everything L. had forgotten. Thirty years had gone by, and my friend didn't remember how she had gotten the job, where the ambassador's apartment was located, or which country he represented. All she recalled was that his native language was English. On the other hand, she remembered his Peruvian wife quite well and told me that the entire staff was white, as was the custom in other African embassies. It struck me as reasonably fair.

The little girls, on the other hand, weren't twins; they were three years apart. The older one was five. With feelings of guilt, humiliation, and fear, L. had witnessed the punishment scene. She resigned shortly afterward, citing personal reasons.

THE URGE FOR A CHILD

In human beings, the desire to reproduce is not an instinctive, biological fact, but rather an intention related to certain social demands, which can appear at any age, or never. And yet, when a woman begins to feel the urge for a child clearly, like a call, very soon this urge becomes a need. Even if it begins as a mental mechanism, a decision that might be considered voluntary, it immediately spreads throughout the whole body and starts to be perceived like a vacuum that pulses in the blood to the rhythm of the heart. There are no cavities in the human body that remain open like caves: the organs settle in, occupying all disposable space; flesh closes in on itself; there are no empty spaces. And yet the woman begins to feel as if a great vortex is passing over her womb, attracting icy winds that cross her from one end to another. She can barely recognize her arms as her own; when she crosses the street she feels them falling uselessly to either side of her body; her breasts ache as if they were stretching, swelling and growing longer; and everything she sees around her becomes a symbol that subjects her to her desire, which locks her within it.

A child. Esmeralda wanted to have a child, and for the first time she began to notice the astonishing number of pregnant women she saw on the street, even in Paris, even in France, where the low birth rate had the nation worried. Even those who didn't look obviously pregnant might have been. Esmé stared enviously at those bulging bellies and scrutinized the faces of the other women, those who had nothing to show off, a certain smile, a certain expression, those always dubious signs, impossible to verify, different for each cultural group, signs that society imagines as typical of the newly-pregnant.

Couples among her friends and acquaintances had suffered the blows of exile. Some had grown closer than ever, while others had broken up and formed new pairings into which, besides Argentines and other Latin Americans, some French people had been introduced, generally from the provinces, with their own air of exiles in the city that attracted people with brute force but welcomed them half-heartedly. Or else French men and women who were the children of exiles, and thus more open to accepting the cultural differences and the flawed, annoying French of the foreigners, their inability to understand certain jokes and puns. Or French people (among whom there might also be children of immigrants or from the provinces), who were fascinated by the exoticism of those Latin Americans, whom they considered so *décontractés*, so free, so cheery, such good dancers, so spontaneous (Chileans, Argentines, Uruguayans: they exchanged amused, surprised looks on hearing this strange description in which they couldn't altogether recognize themselves).

The fact is, both the established, consolidated couples and the new, reconstructed ones were starting to have children; for some, with stability and better jobs their first child arrived, and for others, those who had entered the country with a baby or small child, the second round began, the possibility or necessity of launching a new life into the world, as an act of defiance against all the death they had left behind.

In the minuscule apartment belonging to her friend Bibiana, who had arrived in Paris with her husband a few weeks after them, Esmé picked up the newborn baby, deeply inhaled that odor of vomit and pee, cologne and sweat, the smell of shit and freshly-washed baby clothes, and burst into tears.

JOURNAL ENTRY 4

It won't be long now till my characters leave France. This might be the time to provide some details about my own sojourn in France, which should not be confused with exile. I never was exiled in France (or anywhere else). I never was a militant, not did I have to flee the country for other reasons (and there were plenty of those). My husband and I traveled to Paris in 1976. We lived there for six months, in a studio apartment on Rue Saint-Jacques, in front of the Val-de-Grâce church. We spent an additional three months traveling through Europe and visiting my sister, who already was in exile in Chicago, and in 1977, one of the most terrible years of the dictatorship, we returned to Buenos Aires. We missed it greatly. Nine months spent away from our territory, our language, our world, were enough for us to understand the woes of exile, the unhappiness of being a foreigner, the everyday nostalgia for little things.

In Paris I worked as a reporter and correspondent for the Cambio 16 publishing house, thanks to an Argentine journalist whom we didn't know, but who from that time on and forevermore became a very dear friend. I didn't write for the prestigious Spanish newspaper, however, but rather for an x-rated magazine called *Almanaque*. Franco had died and Spaniards were beginning to discover that sex could be a sin, not just a miracle. I did some investigating for *Almanaque*, writing about the prostitutes' movement in Paris at the time they were fighting for their right to unionize; I wrote about the orgies that were being organized between cars in Place Dauphin; I wrote about porn cinema, which was starting to develop in France, where there was an important production company and several triple-X movie theaters. The Spaniards went wild over porn films: they crossed the border to see films that were forbidden in their own country. We also worked, my husband and I, for a French journalist who didn't write Spanish very well and was a correspondent for a number of Argentine magazines. I acted as ghost writer: I wrote interview questions for her, she gave me the recorded transcripts, and I wrote the articles. My husband took the photos.

ALCIRA AND LEÓN

Guido's parents didn't have the money to visit them in Paris, or maybe they did but preferred to spend it on other things. Guido had many siblings who reproduced, happily and unconscionably, in the city of Santa Fe. Far from the intellectual atmosphere, far from the militancy, they were barely aware of what they would rather not have known. They sent brief, sporadic letters, not much more than greetings, in which they spoke of their work and projects, the birth of their children. Guido's mother's letters began with a brief recap of her illnesses (joint pain, a hiatal hernia, sinusitis), overflowed with references to grandkids and diapers and snotty noses, and never failed to include two or three deadly boring anecdotes in which Guido's nieces and nephews made remarks that only their grandmother could consider clever, unexpected, and even brilliant.

Esmé's mother's letters were devoted, above all, to the weather and the scenery.

It's 68 degrees today, quite cool for December. The sun is hiding, and there are lovely pink and red clouds. Through the window I can see the buildings in the neighborhood, a pretty depressing sight. If I were the mayor, I'd make the condo owners paint the outsides.

And Esmé had no doubt she would get her way. Her mother had a natural talent for exerting authority. At the end there would be some affectionate little phrase from her father, who was unwilling and unable to fill up a page with words that said nothing and who always wrote in capital letters because he was embarrassed by his handwriting.

Illusion, expectation, disappointment, and sadness was the normal sequence with which Guido and Esmé received, opened, and read those letters that arrived (or didn't) in their mailbox three times a day.

That's why Esmé's parents' visit was so unexpected, despite having been announced over and over again. It was their first trip to Europe. They were going to Italy and England and would spend a few days in Paris.

In those days Guido drove an almost-new, metallic blue minivan, recently arrived from Amsterdam, and Esmé, obsessively concerned with her mother's opinion, felt proud to have something to show off. She had carefully cleaned the apartment and was ready to endure nasty or sarcastic remarks, but not the haste with which her mother asked where the refrigerator was and stuck a foil-wrapped package inside. Esmé was glad, at any rate, to have an honest-to-God refrigerator instead of the plastic bag tied to a window railing that had seen them through their first autumn, their first winter in Paris, without needing to run up bills.

"So this is the famous studio," Alcira said.

And even though there was no derision in her voice, Esmé nonetheless sensed that the visit was starting to veer in predictable directions. She felt almost relieved.

"How pretty," León said, indifferently. And he sat down on the bed, which, by day, loaded with throw pillows, turned into a sofa. A thick, black cloth hanging from the ceiling separated the space that Guido devoted to his painting without managing to block the odor that Esmé, practically inured to it, now detected it all its damned pungency.

Only then did Esmé really see her father, whom she had hugged so much that she hadn't been able to really see his face. She was struck by his watery eyes, his protruding belly, his bloated features. He looked old, very old, much older than he actually was, much older than he appeared in the crummy Polaroid photos they sent her from time to time.

"Well, now, where can I boil some water?" Alcira asked.

And while she boiled the syringe and needle, she told Esmé what the carefully described passages in her letters didn't say, what she had never wanted to tell her over the phone during those infrequent, confusing calls, with echoes and noises on the line, which had no purpose other than to offer reassurance that everyone was alive. For over a year they had known that León was a diabetic; it was impossible to control his disease through diet, and he was now insulin-dependent.

"Luckily they put the packet in the fridge on the plane. No, it wasn't luck – because I called the airline in time."

Alcira and León stayed only four days in Paris. Not long at all, but long enough for Esmé to be able to confirm to what point their lives had now become the rest of their lives; that was the extent to which they had been molded by her sister's death. Using all the resources at her disposal, which were considerable, her mother had latched on to reality like a bird of prey latches on to its victim: with those talons. She was focused on living at all costs, on giving meaning to every one of her actions. Her voice was more emphatic, her intelligence was devoted to finding reasons to carry on, to breathe, to get angry, to laugh, to make coffee.

"You've gotta have some fun!" she said.

And with fierce energy she dragged her husband, daughter, and son-in-law to all the activities promoted in the tourist brochures as "musts." In four days Guido and Esmé went to more restaurants than they had experienced in three years; they took a ride in a *bateau-mouche,* one of those little boats that carried tourists along the Seine; they visited museums, palaces, monuments, and even went one night to see the show at the Crazy Horse, where young, naked women did whatever they could to outshine the old tradition of visiting the Lido. (But never, in those four days she shared with them, did Alcira utter the word "grand-child," and that careful, protective, calculated silence made Esmé feel practically like a hopeless case).

"My gynecologist was in Paris. I asked him if he went to the Crazy Horse and he said, 'Naked women? No! I don't work on vacation!'"

Alcira told that story many times, always laughing as though it was the first, but with forced, loud laughter, while her husband joined in as best he could.

Esmé's father, on the other hand, seemed exhausted. His blue eyes, always a little reddened, looked without seeing. The only thing that interested him was food, especially what he wasn't allowed to have. His wife supervised his diet with frenzied obsession, with the same fierce concentration she applied to everything. He concocted all sorts of subterfuges, both simple and complex, to escape that control. Esmé's parents, like any long-married couple, had developed a subtle balance of power. The mother imposed her raging personality, but the father ably deployed the force of his weakness. That complexity, that subtlety, had now grown weaker, simpler, and all the interplay between them had been reduced to a single formula: to eat or not to eat. Of course, every time they sat down in a restaurant, a pitiful scene ensued.

"Choose carefully," Alcira warned him when they handed him the menu.

"You choose," León replied, annoyed.

"You know that's off limits!" Alcira shouted when León's hand started to sneak its way toward the bread basket.

Once she even slapped his hand, which was clasping a slice of warm bread. León dropped the bread, and Esmé, a little frightened, glanced at Guido, who had turned his head and was studiously looking in another direction.

In general, whenever his maneuver was discovered, León would imperceptibly change the direction of his hand to scratch his arm with enthusiasm, as if he'd never meant to do anything else. His entire life force was now concentrated on deceiving his wife whenever he could. Before Esmé's anguished eyes, he waited till her mother went to the bathroom to wolf down a piece of bread. Both of them always carried around some lumps of sugar in case of an attack of hypoglycemia. Alcira checked a couple of times a day to make sure León hadn't eaten them, as sometimes happened.

"Shall we have some coffee together? Just the two of us, you and me? Will you let us, Alcira? Like we used to do?" Esmé's dad proposed on the second day.

Esmé felt a burst of happiness. The two of them went out arm in arm, Esmé so proud of being able to demonstrate to her father her progress in French, her familiarity with the neighborhood, with the chicken vendor (from whom every other day she bought *un petit poulet, coupé en morceaux*), with the waiter at the corner café, with the city. As soon as they walked in, León ordered an ice cream.

"Is that okay, Papá?"

"Sure! I'll just bump up my insulin dose a little, and it'll be fine."

The entire weight of the conversation fell on Esmé. Her father simply stared at the waiter urgently, desperately. When they brought him the ice cream he concentrated on savoring it as if that glass dish contained the meaning of the universe.

"They took away the whole Kamensky family," he said between one spoonful and the next. "Father, mother, two of the kids. One managed to escape to Bolivia and from there to Spain."

"We knew about it. The people who come here bring us news."

With a bit of ice cream in his mouth, León began a process of slow absorption in which his tongue played an important role. On the way home he bought a chocolate *beignet* at the corner bakery and nearly choked trying to finish it before walking into the house.

That night his blood sugar level tested high. Alcira raised his insulin dose a little and gave her daughter an accusing look.

"You didn't watch him!" she said.

"He's an adult, Mamá. Sometimes you seem to forget."

And that little dialogue brought the Big Topic to everyone's attention, the one they had been avoiding, the name that couldn't be pronounced. She, too, was, had been, a young adult. Am I my brother's keeper? My sister's? My daughter's? Nobody had ever blamed Esmé. Alcira and León had carefully avoided blaming one another, and yet all weight of their guilt was there, suffocating them.

And since they didn't mention it, Regina's absence grew greater, sometimes unbearable; it sucked up all the air, all the available oxygen. Once more, as usual, her parents were focused on her sister, Esmé thought. And she had to speak, so that her heart wouldn't burst.

"Do you miss her very much?"

Her mother gazed at her with her wise, deep-set eyes. She stroked her face with painful sweetness, and in her reply she once more revealed herself as demanding, intelligent, wonderful, and terrible, capable of leaping over the fence of words to penetrate the fields of meaning.

"Don't be jealous of the dead, darling," she said, squeezing her hand tightly. "We miss you more, because you could be with us, but you're not."

JOURNAL ENTRY 5

I'm finishing Vasily Grossman's novel, *Life and Fate*, nearly a month after having started it. A thousand pages of war, the Siege of Stalingrad, Stalinism, denunciations. But at the same time, and in contrast with its content, from an artistic point of view it's a Stalinist novel: social realism at its purest. A large, powerful novel, strangely old-fashioned. A total novel in which the narrator not only knows everything about the protagonists, but also *tells everything*, absolutely everything. So many characters and situations that I can barely remember them. Some I've forgotten completely and can't quite recognize when the author takes them up again; others barely occupy one page and yet they can easily be identified by their physical appearance, their personality, their past and their future.

That's not the novel I'd like to write, despite the respect it provokes in me. I'm more inclined toward elision, ambiguity, a few brushstrokes that let you guess the rest. But I can't help wondering why it's so hard for me to name my characters, and when I do, I almost feel as if I'm betraying myself. What's the problem? Why don't my characters have a face; why don't I want to describe them physically (considering that I'm obviously capable of doing so). Guido and Esmé still don't have a last name. Should I choose a Jewish surname? Italian? Neutral? And in each case, why? Suddenly I understand that my protagonist's sister isn't called Gloria, as I had decided at first, but Regina. The name struck me on the spur of the moment, as I was riding the subway, as an absolute necessity. The computer easily makes these changes.

But, most of all, what to tell? I ask myself at each step; writing is that *unnatural*. Should I write more about the couple, Guido and Esmé? Should I talk about their sexual relations, their evolution, their fantasies? What gives each of them pleasure, what are their disappointments, what is it that each one expects, uselessly, of the other? Should the reader know if Esmé is tall or short, the color of her eyes, her childhood memories? Do I need to write about her religious beliefs? Is it possible to tell EVERYTHING? Should I take it all on?

THE DECISION

Esmé and Guido are walking along Rue de l'Harpe, twisting and shiny. It's nighttime; a brisk chill reddens their cheeks. The street is filled with young people waiting in line to get into the movies and fill the bistros. They're happy to be living in Paris. The air smells like crêpes and roasted chestnuts.

"Liliana tells me that in Seattle people shut themselves in at home after five PM. Empty streets. Nobody walks. Even if you're only going three blocks, you take the car," Esmé says.

"Here, in any crummy little dive bar, the food is delicious. If your order fries, what fries they are!" says Guido, climbing aboard the wave of satisfaction.

The chill is more than brisk, and the temperature has remained the same all day. At dawn it was 38 degrees. At noon, with the sky as cloudy as ever, it was still 38; at mid-afternoon it was 38, and now, at about 11 PM, it's approximately 38. Over the course of several years, instead of acclimating, Esmé feels the cold more and more.

"Don't you ever feel it?" she persists.

"Don't I ever feel what?" Guido asks, as if he didn't know.

"The urge. To have kids."

"Yes, but it passes, you know? Because … what if later

on I get tired and change my mind, but the deed is done? We've talked it over a thousand times, Esmé. The urge will come, but I still don't feel …"

"You don't have to feel anything. It's something that happens. It's part of nature."

"But you and I don't believe in nature, Esmé. We're human beings, cultured beings, aren't we? I think of the word FATHER and I see it in capital letters, so great, so important …"

"Not because of your father, that's for sure," Esmé jabs.

"Because of the father I'd like to be," Guido sidesteps.

A sudden gust of wind gives Esmé, who has lost this skirmish, but not the war, enough footing to change the subject.

"*Moi* cold, *moi!*" she moans.

"Put on my jacket," says Guido, lovingly, paternally, compensatorily.

Esmé assesses Guido's coat; in addition to his long underwear and flannel undershirt, he's wearing two sweaters and a scarf. All right, she can accept the jacket without inflicting serious harm on her husband's health. They're approaching their studio apartment and again congratulate each other on the happiness that Paris gives them. She rejoices because everything is so lovely, because the city's beauty crosses their path and it's not necessary to seek it out: you can be anywhere, you look around, and there it is: beautiful! He thinks of the many parts of the city that have nothing beautiful about them, but he doesn't say so; he knows that she knows, too. So he rejoices aloud, praising the artistic stimulus, what it means to live in a city where you can find people from every corner of the world to exchange glances and interests with.

Esmé snuggles into Guido's jacket, sticks her hand in the pocket, and feels a discomfiting, surprising little package. A rectangular package. She takes it out, looks at it. It's a package of condoms. She shakes it distractedly. The latex rounds, each in its little plastic wrapper, bump against the package, producing a dull sound. It's still a few years before the height of the AIDS era; for the time being condoms are used only to avoid pregnancy in emergency situations. Esmé uses a diaphragm, with the damn spermicidal ointment that works like a breeding ground for yeast infections, which in turn obliges her to insert fungicidal capsules. The diaphragm is supposed to remain in place for ten hours after having sexual relations. Esmé hates it. Now she picks up the little box and displays it in horror.

"What the hell …"

"No, it's nothing, it's because … It's just that … I wanted to surprise you!"

"Well, you have!"

"I mean … It's for you. Because you always complain about the diaphragm, right? So I thought we might switch … methods, I mean. Ha-ha. To go back to the source … To the old-fashioned way!"

But she's not smiling. She doesn't seem grateful for Guido's consideration, for his nice gift. Another icy gust sets her ashiver inside the jacket. She doesn't say anything. She can't think of anything to say. Despite the gloves, her hands are cold, but she doesn't dare stick them in the pockets again. She looks at Guido intently, like a painter studying his model's face.

"But, you know what?" Suddenly inspired, Guido switches tactic. "We won't need them anymore!"

He snatches the little box from her hands and unceremoniously tosses it into a drain.

"Because we're going to have a child," he assures her enthusiastically.

"Really?" Esmé is almost afraid to believe it.

"Really. You're right. I need to grow up once and for all. It's time."

"Here? In Paris? A French kid?"

"No, of course not. Do you want a French kid? One who'll be born with round little frameless glasses?"

"And skinny lips!" For the first time since the discovery, Esmé laughs.

Paris is a beautiful place, without a doubt, but they're fed up with being foreigners. They miss Buenos Aires. They even miss those things about Buenos Aires that they hated or pretended to hate. The broken sidewalks with cracked tiles. The smell of pizza. The trees: those trees, and no others. The taxi drivers, always curious, always in the mood to chat. The people. Their loved ones in particular and the people of Buenos Aires in general.

And so, in no more than a couple of words, they've just made some basic life decisions. To have a child, to return to Argentina. They've discussed it before. With the Falklands War lost, the dictatorship is crumbling. Guido, who never was a militant, and Esmé, who was a bit player in university militant circles, no longer feel endangered.

Once more the cold feels upbeat, stimulating. Again, Esmé gazes intently at Guido's face, but in a completely different way, as if she were trying to read those features which their child, as yet made only of words, will inherit. As they embrace and kiss, Esmé tries to forget that the little box of condoms was open and nearly empty.

JOURNAL ENTRY 6

Doubts, doubts, doubts. I want to tell this story from Esmé's point of view. Should I opt for the first person? I really like the first person. I'm fascinated by its limits, everything it doesn't know. The first person doesn't see beyond its visual field. It doesn't know (we don't know) what others think or feel. Besides, I believe that choosing it would allow me to enrich the character with a particular tone of voice, give me more freedom to delve into her memory.

In a way, because of its tone and the time when it takes place, this novel has been, until now, almost a continuation of another novel of mine, *The Loves of Laurita*. *Laurita* is narrated in the third person, although the confessional effect is so overwhelming that no one realizes it. Until now, I've only used the first person for those novels that are told from a man's perspective, *Patient* and *Death as a Side Effect*. By some law of perversity, that stratagem allows me to separate them more from myself.

Autbiographical elements: yes, there are some, but the reader doesn't need to know which ones they are.

If I finally decide on the first person and rewrite the whole thing from that point of view, what will I do with this text?

The Quest

Once upon a time there was a king and a queen who couldn't have a child, and only in polygamous cultures was male sterility made public. In all other cultures, the woman was the only one responsible. Guaraní shamans made women eat frog powder; the Sioux stuck phallus-shaped stones inside them; in Asia and Africa remedies such as tiger liver, claws, and bones or rhinoceros horn were used. The Egyptians recommended pouring sand with milk over the woman's body while the man penetrated her. The Greeks imagined that when the neck of the uterus was too tightly closed, it was possible to open it with a mixture of red saltpeter, cumin, resin, and honey. They also used a technique that consisted of dilating the cervix and inserting a lead pipe in the uterus, through which they spilled emollients. In Rome, young patrician women flocked to Juno's temple to ensure pregnancy. Naked and prostrate, they were flagellated by acolytes of the god Pan with whips made of he-goat hide. In the 13th century, Valencian doctor Arnau de Villanova inserted a clove of garlic into the vagina; if the odor reached the woman's mouth, her fertility was confirmed. Female frigidity was as much a culprit as excessive desire. In the sixteenth century, Ambroise Paré insisted on dilation of the cervix. Hebrew women followed and revered the miraculous *tzadikim;* Hindu women followed and revered dervishes; Christian women prayed to the saints, the Virgin, the Lord. All of them listened reverently to canticles and spells designed to restore their fertility: they tied red wool to stones, they kissed snakes; they locked themselves indoors and fasted during menstruation; they drank or inserted potions that were sometimes harmless and sometimes as dangerous as the one that killed Eusebia, Empress of Byzantium. Once upon a time there was a king and a queen who couldn't have a child, and the awareness of this reality, even though it had taken shape slowly over the years, always caught them by surprise. They thought it so incredible, so unexpected, so unfair.

For Esmé the hysterosalpingogram is the worst. She's on a cot with her legs spread and tied, while the doctor vigorously injects the contrast dye (painful) into the neck of the uterus (painful), fills the uterus itself (painful) and advances – or should advance – laboriously – through the fallopian tubes, causing her the most extreme pain she's ever felt in her life. She lets out an uncontrollable scream and her eyes cloud over. The doctor hides behind the lead partition that (unfairly?) protects his own genitals. Esmé hears the click of the x-ray machine. Then they admit Guido, who strokes her forehead, terrified. Esmé doesn't quite faint. Now she sits up a little and vomits on the floor.

Hysterosalpingogram is the ridiculous name (which she'll never forget) for an x-ray of the uterus and fallopian tubes, and it is without a doubt the worst thing – so far. Much worse than the minor indignity of taking her temperature rectally every morning. Much worse than answering Dr. Silverberg's invasive questions. For a while

Esmé believed that there was nothing worse than forgetting or shunting aside the main function of sex, which
is pleasure, and turning it into a chore, a duty regulated
by the line of mercury in the thermometer, desire transformed into obligation, with all intensity and temblor
focused on the result. For a while she thought that it was
even worse to start feeling the symptoms, tension in her
breasts, pain in her thighs, spasms in her lower belly,
trying not to lose her illusions, trying to convince herself that the symptoms of pregnancy are so similar to this,
that's how they are, just the same, trying to convince herself that those first drops of blood, on precisely that date,
could be due to embryonic implantation, and don't many
women keep menstruating for a while or sometimes even
throughout their pregnancies, but not Esmé, not her, and
so the blood, traditional, brownish at first, then gradually
turning redder as the flow increases, later the clots, and
her illusion turns into shreds, disappointment, sadness, her
illusion is destroyed once more in the ancient wellspring
of her blood.

But the hysterosalpingogram is worse yet. The only
advantage is that it isn't repeated. Esmé harbors the hope
(she goes from hope to hope) that insufflation, an injection of carbon dioxide, won't be necessary, at that moment in the history of medicine, to determine if her
fallopian tubes are open or blocked and to unblock them
if necessary. To examine the uterine horns, the place
where the uterus and the fallopian tubes are joined. Ah,
what a symphony can be found in her uterine horns! In
Peter and the Wolf (her parents made her listen to it over
and over when she was a child, with the firm determina-

tion of awakening her latent musical ability) the horns are sinister, threatening, terrible: they represent the wolf.

Guido and Esmé showed up for the first time at Dr. Silverberg's office almost convinced that it was a premature visit. After all, it had been only six months that they'd been trying, fruitlessly, for the child that they had scrupulously avoided having until then. However, the doctor wasn't concerned with their six months of trying, but rather, offensively, their two years of marriage. He called them an "infertile couple," and the shameful label, which they never would have applied to themselves, the name that united them in their failure, was what he wrote down in their file.

And yet the sluggishness with which the diagnosis proceeded soon made Esmé aware that, above all, it was a matter of letting that mysterious entity which apparently was impossible to attribute to human beings – old, scoffed-at, incomprehensible nature – do her work. Medicine couldn't do much if nature didn't want to cooperate. The not-so-reliable temperature arc was the only way to know if ovulation had taken place. Esmé had to get used to staying in bed when she awoke until she had inserted the thermometer, waited a couple of minutes, and recorded the results. Three months were consumed in calculating the arc, in making note of the length of her cycles. During that first phase of their consultation, only the woman was studied. When the woman was young, the tests, x-rays, and studies went slowly, one visit after another, allowing time for chance or luck. Or nature. Many months, possibly years, later, the doctors would order a sperm count.

Like any woman, like queens, peasants, and slaves, like millions of women throughout history, Esmé plodded through the labyrinths of science, through pain, indignity, and punishments, buoyed by that will, perhaps biological, that now seemed to occupy her entire life: the urge for a child.

The hysterosalpingogram is the worst part, but it's also the most effective. The result shows that the uterus is intact, free of adhesions or flaps. One of the fallopian tubes is blocked. The other has probably been unblocked by the contrast dye. Insufflation is unnecessary because a few days after the test, Esmé is pregnant.

Journal Entry 7

A utopia narrates or describes a wonderful, perfect society. A dystopia's theme is the worst of all possible worlds. A uchronia proceeds along alternate and contemporary timelines: what might our world be like, for instance, if the Nazis had won the Second World War. This novel is beginning to take on the shape of a sort of personal uchronia, an alternative autobiography. What might have happened to me if. Although her story may differ from mine, my character, Esmé, rather resembles her author's *alter ego* (not me, exactly, since I'm nothing more than yet another *alter ego*, similar and dishonest).

Some of the difficulties I run into (I fall, get up, plod laboriously onward): once again, as usual, I know what the characters say; I can relate what's happening to them, explain or show their interactions. On the other hand, it's impossible for me to describe places, objects, atmospheres in my first draft. At first my characters are nowhere, like those children's drawings where, lacking a horizon line or objects to tie them to earth, the stick figures seem to be floating on the sheet of paper. Luckily, I'm aware of this deficit, and in the second draft I add some of the elements necessary to situate the characters, to connect them to the world around them.

Guido and Esmé still don't have a last name. In my first novel, the protagonist didn't even have a first name. Ah, what a pleasure! He didn't need one.

Back Home

While she had been trying diligently and secretly for a child, Esmé returned to her old job as advertising copy writer, from which she had boasted of freeing herself, but which in fact she missed greatly. If only she had known enough French to work in an advertising agency in France. On loose sheets of paper that she never showed anyone, not even Guido, Esmé tried to create commercial ads and copy of the kind she attentively studied in French magazines and newspapers. But a good commercial ad requires a command of the language that includes an awareness of its levels, the differences between written and oral language, formal register and street slang, familiarity with those words that were in vogue during the previous generation, neologisms assimilated by the very young, knowledge of children's lullabies, sayings and proverbs, popular songs, the subtle combination of wordplay and a feel for history and culture that can't be acquired in just a few years, something that a foreigner might never acquire at all.

After the Falklands War, thanks, perhaps, to the Falklands War, the dictatorship was crumbling. The last general who had assumed the presidency found himself obliged to call for elections. At last, after many years, political propaganda once again covered flyers on the walls of the city. Newspapers, radio, television, were saturated with politics.

When dealing with politics, the word isn't *publicity*, but *propaganda*. Political parties or their candidates pay up front because the agencies (and the media and film producers and photographers and the whole flock of little vampires who feed on political blood during an election year) have to make sure they get paid, even if the candidate or the party loses the election.

Esmé started to work in an agency again, forming part of a team dedicated to handling a political account, a very small party, practically a family, but one with a long history and illusions of power. Several brothers would meet, sitting around their patriarch, a big-shot economist who bragged of having been able to swiftly detect and denounce every one of the economic-political sinkholes into which the country had fallen by not listening to his prophetic words in time. He wanted the electoral campaign to hinge around that topic, where they felt solid. It was useless to try to convince them that people don't vote for gloom-and-doom-mongers. Besides (and this could not be mentioned), no prophet of catastrophes and calamities in Argentina had ever been wrong. The father, brothers, cousins, and other relatives and friends who, in effect, made up the party, were very intelligent people with whom it was a pleasure to chat on any other subject, but who were strangely blind when it came to the political arena, although they were very well placed in terms of economic power. The excellent relationship between the party's leadership and the country's big businesses permitted a constant flow of money that fed the bountiful, but baffling, electoral race. Many executives of those businesses were convinced of the utility of contributing large sums to the party's campaign, in part because they contributed to *all* parties' campaigns, and in part because they were people with sufficient power and connections to benefit the business even if they didn't win the elections, but especially because the advertising agency kicked back a large percentage of those sums, which would end up in their overseas private accounts.

Meanwhile, the patriarch and his sons seem to have placed limitless confidence in the owner of the advertising agency, who seduced them with his physical appearance: tall, with the face of a Roman soldier and a prematurely white mane, the man knew how to make his victims fall in love with him and surrender as gleefully as a male praying mantis to his ravenous mate.

The campaign team included two writers and a psychologist who specialized in polls and market research. The owner of the company in charge of filming the short TV campaign ads was also running for the legislature. With his dyed yellow hair and his dandyish, Buenos Aires lounge lizard demeanor (bordering on parody), he swiftly produced, according to the demands of the agency (which had concrete interests in every one of the productions), an endless series of films that gradually formed the worst electoral campaign of the year, but which was, thanks to a clever combination of factors, the most expensive.

While Esmé returned to advertising, like someone who goes back to an old lover whom she never wanted to let go, Guido abandoned the law altogether, like someone who shrugs off a misguided, youthful love affair once and for all. But in Buenos Aires it made no sense to keep pretending to be a painter, either. Before leaving Paris, he sold almost all his easels, brushes, spatulas, oils, and canvases, in a kind of jumble sale, to his friends.

The smuggling of minivans from Amsterdam had brought him a small sum in francs that would begin to have some importance in Argentina now that the madness of "easy money," that delusional idea imposed by the dictatorship and later repeated by certain democratic governments, was over, the idea that the Argentine peso could be stronger, more optimistic, healthier, and most of all, have more buying power than the dollar. Using that money, he partnered with a friend who wanted to start up a modest textile business.

Faithful, as always, to the theoretical development of his interests, Guido soon became a Real Entrepreneur. Smiling tolerantly and understandingly at his own adolescent missteps, he got rid of the casual, eternally paint-spattered clothes that he had worn in Paris, and started demanding that his shirts be carefully ironed. He switched from marijuana to Lexotan, became unexpectedly punctual, and bought an impressive number of ties.

Journal Entry 8

From Erri de Luca, an Italian writer:

> As the pages grow longer, I'm annoyed that I can't recall the girl's name. A fifty-year hiatus is no excuse. Sentences about her come into my head as I advance; specific details are added, but nothing about her name. I could foist some arbitrary name on her, something from Greek mythology, but I'd turn into just another practitioner of the trade, someone who invents things.
>
> As a reader, I immediately forget the names in a story. They don't add consistency, and they're a convention. And so I leave the space for the name blank and continue to call her the girl, because I didn't meet her when she was a child.

The book is called *Fish Don't Close Their Eyes*. Erri de Luca elegantly validates my difficulties. If Luca himself, as a reader, immediately forgets the names in a story, why go to the trouble of inventing them?

Of course de Luca is relating his memories (or pretending to). In this case, I am *just another practitioner of the trade, someone who invents*. I have the right to give them whatever first and last names I like. Or to leave them nameless if I prefer. In his infinite search for *lost time*, Proust mentions his main character's name only once.

THE OLYMPIC CHALLENGE

Esmé thought that the days when her sister's death was a living, searing burn were behind her. She didn't realize that her years in exile had concealed or weakened or postponed certain stages of grief.

Regina had never been with her in Paris, and nothing in Paris reminded Esmé of her. Only now, in Buenos Aires, could she measure the impact of her absence, which was everywhere. In the square where they had played and grown up together, in the cafés where they met toward the end, in the streets, on buses, at the movies, in dreams, and especially at her parents' house. There was the red armchair where she used to make her sit with her eyes closed, so that she could push her around and play Ghost Train. There was the Donald Duck cup, the only one from which Regina would condescend to drink her milk. There were the green-and-white striped comforters, with ruffles, that covered the twin beds in the room they had shared. And there was Regina, ponderous, unbearable, and apparently, immovable, until Esmé's belly began to swell. Only at that moment, so slowly that at first it was impossible to notice, did the monotonous presence of her absence begin to fade.

Although the pregnancy seemed eternal and marvelous, a state of grace that had no reason to change (Esmé and perhaps Guido, were so afraid of what would come later), everything that begins must also come to an end at some point. And so it was that one night Esmeralda found herself feeling contractions (so *that's* what those famous contractions were like!) every ten minutes, as Guido, watch in hand, took notes and made calculations.

The overnight bag for the hospital had been ready for days. Guido and Esmé, who had diligently and faithfully attended pre-natal classes, felt like athletes, marathon runners who, after nine months of fierce training, had finally arrived at the moment of their Olympic challenge. Now or never! Esmé panted with joyful enthusiasm every time a contraction came, while Guido massaged her back and panted along with her, trying to match her rhythm, though much more often than necessary. Both of them panted, rhythmically, happily; the contractions came every ten minutes and were hardly painful at all.

Guido phoned the doctor, who asked to speak to Esmeralda and calmed them even more by reassuring them that they – he and the midwife – were at their beck and call, ready to leave at a moment's notice, and that they should call back when the contractions were coming every three minutes or if there was any other news.

"What other news?" Guido asked, his voice trembling a little.

"The mucus plug," said Esmé, who had studied rigorously.

"I forgot. I forgot what happens with the mucus plug."

"It's expelled," said Esmeralda.

"And is that normal? Will you know when it happens?"

"It's normal and I'll know. My water might break, too."

"Don't tell me. I don't want to know."

"It's nothing, Guido. They explained it to us. At this point it's nothing serious."

"I don't like the idea of anything breaking in the Fish Tank."

At that point the baby's sex was still a mystery, but meanwhile they had grown accustomed to calling it the Little Perch. And Esmé's belly was, of course, the Fish Tank. As it still wasn't possible to determine the baby's sex with certainty before birth, the grandmothers had given them an astonishing quantity of baby clothes in shades of mint green, white, and ducky yellow. When the contractions started coming every six minutes, they also became more painful.

Then the lights went out. This happened fairly regularly, and it lasted between ten minutes and three days. Guido and Esmé's apartment was on the fifteenth floor.

"Tell the doctor we're going to check into the hospital," Esmé said between one contraction and another. "I can still walk down the stairs; later it'll be harder."

Guido went on ahead, carrying the bag in one hand and holding the flashlight in the other. Esmé leaned on his shoulders, carefully descending step by step in the darkness. It was two AM, the super was asleep, and no one had taken the trouble of putting candles on the landings between staircases. It was a long, slow journey that sped up the frequency of the contractions. On the second floor there was a candle. Between the first floor and the lobby, there were wax drippings.

"If you slip, I'll kill you!" Guido said, and it was a threat made out of love.

But Esmé slipped. How, exactly, does a fall happen? A slow-motion camera can show it in detail, but for the person falling it's practically a mystery. It takes place frame by frame, and yet it's still incomprehensible: how and why did that foot extend beyond the edge of the step; how and why did the hands that were gripping Guido's shoulder fail to maintain her balance; how and why didn't she grab the banister to keep from falling? Luckily there were only a few steps left to go, and Guido's legs wedged in between, preventing her from rolling. There was Esmé, suddenly on the ground, and although she had the sensation of falling very slowly, she couldn't possibly have reconstructed or comprehended what happened. Pain, pain. She had impacted her entire body, her head too, though not so much, and her belly as well, and yet it wasn't the pain of the fall that was making her scream, a contained scream, a controlled moan, but rather the violence of a contraction that left her incapable of feeling anything else.

In the hospital room, Esmé surrendered entirely to the pain; she stopped pretending she could bear it. They were on a lower floor, with a view of the outdoors. Like in the movies (and what is life, anyway, but a poor imitation of Hollywood), she hung on to the bars on the headboard so as to ride out the contractions, and she screamed, ear-splitting screams, shamelessly out of control.

"Pant, darling, pant!" Guido said, terrified, holding her hands during the increasingly brief pauses between contractions, as if in the ocean of pain that engulfed

Esmé there was any other way to breathe than by panting. And he panted, too, out of solidarity and to set a good example, to mark the rhythm that Esmé was forgetting, because her disorganized panting responded to the internal rhythm of pain that had taken over her entire body, her entire mind, and seemed to have no connection with the birth of her baby, which by now was no more than a very distant probability that she could hardly remember.

Suddenly, like a couple of TV cops, the doctor and the midwife flung open the door and entered the room, almost violently. No doubt the screams could be heard from the street. The doctor checked her dilation and ordered an injection to eliminate unproductive contractions, while the midwife showed her how to manage the pain. She spoke to her in a calm, firm voice, and at last Esmé understood that the whole package of instructions, exercises, and supposedly natural techniques that the laboring woman was supposed to learn and apply had not been so clearly intended for her, to assuage or control her pain, but rather were at the service of those around her. It was a matter of avoiding those unpleasant, disturbing screams, in reality the body's most natural and obvious reaction, the simplest way to unload and, to a certain extent, relieve the sensation of splitting in two, which was exactly what was happening to her. In two. Only at that moment she couldn't and didn't want to remember the part of her belly that was about to become another person. Now she understood and envied those indigenous women, whom she imagined as isolated in the jungle, delivering peacefully, alone, squatting, perhaps with another woman at their side, screaming to their heart's content.

And in spite of it all, her obstetrician was so modern, so generous, that he spared her the habitual practice, the additional torture, of the enema. There was hardly any time between the contractions when the doctor decided that the time had come to proceed to the delivery room.

"Do you want anesthesia, Esmé?" the doctor asked.

"What a question! Of course I want it!" Esmé panted, nearly indignant. "You're the one that has to decide!"

A nurse gave her the epidural injection. First it was the fear of the needle penetrating between her vertebrae, then a strange, painful feeling. Like a slow, enormous whirlpool, the liquid entered the epidural space between the spinal cord and the vertebrae, entered God-knows-where, into a part of her body that didn't exist, that until that moment had never existed.

In those days, fathers – some fathers – were beginning to participate in childbirth, with the permission of the doctors – some doctors. Guido was already decked out in white scrubs, with his cap and mask on, when a fainting spell convinced him that it would be better not to go into the delivery room. Esmé was grateful. Now she only had to worry about herself, and yet they didn't let her (how horrid it would have been to be screaming alone, squatting, in the middle of the jungle). The midwife and the nurses placed her in the gynecological position, her feet supported by stirrups, which at least allowed her to push and support herself whenever the need to push arose, as it did now. She could hardly feel her legs, but she did feel the contractions, though they weren't painful. Push, push, said many voices around her, now push again, as if it were possible not to, as if her womb wasn't the one that decided to push with all its might in order to expel once and for all that strange body, which now, for the first time, was ceasing to be part of her own.

They placed the baby, panting and dirty, on her chest. The two of them were exhausted and, perhaps, happy. Then they took her away to show her to her daddy and grandparents. Then Esmé expelled the placenta. Then something began to change tone in the delivery room, the voices growing sharper, a certain urgency, and Esmé understood that all was not well. Then, as the doctor carried out certain incomprehensible maneuvers, which she partially saw without feeling anything because she was still anesthetized, the midwife explained that there was a small hemorrhage.

"Don't worry," she said. "It happens sometimes. Your uterus is a little lazy; it doesn't want to contract like it should. We're giving you oxytocin to stimulate the contractions."

A few hours later Esmé was nearly out of danger, receiving a transfusion, in intensive care. The only way to stop the hemorrhage that had threatened to carry her off was by removing her uterus.

Her daughter was incredibly beautiful and would never have siblings.

Journal Entry 9

My agent, my friends, a colleague, a journalist, all ask about what I'm writing. What is this project that I'm devoting so much time to and that keeps me from making other commitments? They ask me more out of politeness than curiosity, to demonstrate their interest in my work. I try changing the subject. It's a mistake to talk about what one is writing. A project doesn't exist, it's nothing, till it's finished, and that's even truer when it comes to a novel. Once I wrote a piece of flash fiction on this topic:

> A writer describes the idea for a story that he's about to write. He tells it at a table in a café, and the idea is good. The air grows tense around his word; the story becomes so tangible that the cigarette smoke can't penetrate it; their spirals form the border of its transparent outline. But later, when he tries to turn it into letters, he detects cracks he hadn't noticed before, which the words slip through; a haze of banality invades the text, and the Gods reject the offering of a victim who is no longer pure, whom others have enjoyed before Them.

And yet, it's hard to contain oneself. It's so much easier, more enjoyable, so much less of a commitment to tell the story than to write it. It creates the false illusion that it already exists, that only a little patience is needed, it's just a question of sitting at the keyboard for a sufficient length of time to give it its place in the world, but it's not true, of course: a literary project is nothing, nothing more than air and lies. The struggle against the words is what will define its existence, and if the words win, if it's impossible to defeat them, dominate them; the idea will return to chaos, from which it never should have emerged. The temptation is great, and, committing the error of giving in to it, I told a colleague about the tragic birth of Guido and Esmé's daughter.

"But that doesn't happen anymore," he said to me, self-confidently. "These days there are no post-partum hemorrhages that science can't control. Taking out her uterus! Unrealistic."

And yet I didn't invent the situation; I couldn't have. I have no imagination. I'm completely incapable of inventing anything. All I know how to do is to combine, more or less logically, bits of what I extract from reality. I know the protagonist in real life; I know about that terrible hemorrhage that nearly carried her off and ended her possibility of having more children. I prefer first-hand information and would have loved to interview her, maybe record her. But in this case, the circumstances were tragic enough for discretion (mine) to prevent any kind of investigation. I found the rest of the information on the Internet. After all, that's what it's for.

The fact is, now that the newborn baby girl exists in my story. I can't blame anyone but myself. I myself gave her life and now, damn it all, I have to give her a name, too.

GUILT

Thus began the worst kind of guilt for Esmé, the kind that feeds on itself, the guilt that has no limits and cannot be controlled: the deep guilt of always feeling guilty and therefore of finding herself in a situation of weakness, fragility, which turns the guilty party into someone terribly easy to manipulate, a puppet that's ready to dance to the tune of anyone who's able to pick up on her doubts, her fears, her constant, exhausting, inexhaustible, and boring guilt complex. The guilt of being a mother.

It all started so quickly, so unexpectedly. She had barely left the intensive care unit and been taken to her room, where her mother awaited her in sunglasses and a mask. Esmé was very weak and it frightened her a little.

"Mamá! Why is your face covered up?"

"I had to put on the mask because you're anemic. Your resistance is very low."

"No one else wears a mask … Not even in Intensive Care."

"But I'm your mother, Esmé. I love you more."

"And the sunglasses? Here? Inside?"

"They're so you won't notice I've been crying. Now they're going to bring in your baby, and you'll have to get ready for her. You need to take off your nightgown and hold her against your skin. It's very important, on account of those two days when you were apart. That's what Gloria said."

Gloria was Alcira's psychologist. She had helped her after her daughter's death. Alcira took her word as Gospel.

"Where's Guido?"

"I sent him out for coffee. This has to be just between mother and daughter. And the baby will stay in your room with you so she'll start to notice you. You'll have to nurse her," said Alcira in an exaggeratedly gentle, but demanding, voice.

"Mamá, go find him, please. I want him to be with me. I feel terrible. I've just come from Intensive Care. I can't be in charge of anything."

"I'll help you."

"Please, Mamá!"

And while her mother, with her face covered by that strange mask, went out to look for Guido, Esmé was alone for a moment and realized that she didn't know what she was doing there. By making an effort, she could remember why she had gone to the hospital, but she felt in a way as if she'd forgotten about it, or that it wasn't so important anymore. Now she was feeling a little better, and the only thing she wanted was to recover altogether and then go back home, she and her husband. No one else. For everything to be the same as usual. Who was she, what was she, and where had that baby come from (and she looked at her body, taken aback, at that still-swollen, prominent belly), that baby everyone now wanted to foist off on her so that she could take care of it, when she wasn't even in any condition to take care of herself?

Many times she had returned to that strange feeling, that initial, terrible guilt, that involuntary rejection of motherhood, which would disappear a few hours later, as soon as she held Natalia in her arms, against her skin, the two of them alone, and she was able to give her the damn bottle, the plastic and rubber contraption that was going to separate them, insinuating itself between the two of them. She had so wanted to be able to feed her from her own body, to bond with her daughter in that loving, sensual encounter, to insert her milk-heavy breast into her daughter's mouth. But it had been forbidden. The anemia caused by the hemorrhage, plus the load of antibiotics that she had received, made each of them, Esmé and her daughter, toxic to one another. Her daughter, Natalia Regina: after a vigorous discussion with her husband, Esmé understood that Regina should be the child's middle name, the one that's represented by an initial; she understood that she mustn't burden the baby with the dead woman's weight.

Was it then that it all began? Was it that uncontrollable, but fleeting, rejection of what she had most wanted in life? She was to ask herself that question many times.

"Your little girl has leadership qualities," a nurse told her, much later, when she had had already held her against her body, on top of her body, in her body, and even later she would proudly recall that remark, which at the time had seemed so terrible: "She bursts out crying and all the others follow in chorus!"

And how she cried! When they took her back to the nursery at night, she cried! Esmé asked them to leave the baby in the room with her, but her doctor was inflexible:

during the day, all right, but at night the new mother had to rest, regain her strength. For Esmé, imagining her daughter far away and crying was like physical torture, compounding the many other pains (birth, episiotomy, the operation to remove her uterus) that assailed her, in spite of the tranquilizers.

And no doubt something did begin at that moment, the feeling that devastated her for a long time, for the rest of her life, a feeling of terror and obsession related to the many sufferings that lay in wait for her daughter, along with the hideous dangers of life and of the world. To live was terrible; to live was to bear, constantly, on your back and in your guts, the seed of death. Her baby was so fragile, so delicate, so weak, so exposed … How would she hold on to her when she was able to stand with Natalia in her arms? How do you hold a baby? How and why doesn't it fall from its mother's arms?

"Like a radio," said her mother-in-law, who had come from Santa Fe to meet her thousandth granddaughter. She herself had had seven children with cheerful simplicity. "A new-born baby is like a radio. You pick it up like this, see? Like it's a radio. It makes lots of noise, but it doesn't move; wherever you put it, that's where it stays."

JOURNAL ENTRY 10

I would have liked to narrate one section in the first person, to separate it from the rest, a section in which Esmé thinks about her daughter, trying to replay her life, trying to figure out where she went wrong. In short, that inventory of fault into which we mothers all plunge every time we have doubts (more often than necessary) about what we did for/to/against our children. But if this very common, almost traditional, angst is narrated in the first person, I run the risk of mixing and confusing it with these comments. When I made the decision to write this diary, I renounced the first person completely for the rest of the novel, no exceptions. On the other hand, the notion of recapitulation vanished quickly. Flashbacks annoy me a little, and so I chose to keep moving forward in chronological order.

What do readers care about my choices? Why would my doubts interest them? But, if we follow this line of reasoning to its ultimate consequences, why would they be interested in my novel at all, this one or any other? Why do they read fiction? Isn't it better to limit oneself, as the vast majority of people do today, to textbooks and acquiring information, and when the body demands fiction (because it does), to limit oneself to audiovisual entertainment? Isn't it so much easier to be moved by a good actress's face than by the words that describe her anguish? Isn't it much easier to accompany her feigned tears with one's own sincere, but facile, empathic, painless ones? And yet, without words, what are we? Less than an olive, as the Talmud would say, where the size of an olive is the limit of what is forbidden (everything smaller than an olive is permissible). Less than a sesame seed, according to *The Thousand and One Nights.* Less than nothing.

THE FIRST YEARS

Happiness is an elusive lady. She likes the art of disguise and hides her pleasant, composed face behind a veil so as not to be recognized, so that no one will know she was there, so that wretched human beings will be obliged to look backward, to prod their memories, always uncertain, trying to reconstruct the tableau of their recollections to ask themselves: Do you remember? She was there, but we didn't recognize her! That was happiness! For her parents, Natalia's first years were pure happiness disguised as minor setbacks. It took them many years to understand this.

Was Natalia objectively as beautiful as Esmé supposed? What was her daughter really like, Esmé wondered? How did others see her? During the first days she could barely take her eyes off her, partly because she was enraptured by her beauty, her existence, her tiny face, her body, her hands, and especially her feet, so perfect and poignant that they sometimes made her cry, and partly because she felt that her motherly gaze was what sustained the fragile movement of her breath. How could she be sure, totally sure, that her daughter would keep breathing when she stopped gazing at her?

By the time they returned home, Esmé was able to stand and change the baby, though all her movements were slow and required terrible effort. The first time she went out into the street, the corner seemed so far away, on the other side of the world. She couldn't imagine walking such a distance. At first Guido timed how long it took them to heat the bottle, to feed Natalia, to burp and change her. The time was cut in half as Esmé recovered and practiced. She waited for Guido to come home at night so they could bathe her together. She was afraid that the baby might slip and drown in the tub.

Her grandmother cut her nails for the first time, and Esmé found the operation agonizing. Her anxiety was almost uncontrollable. Those tiny fingers, so tender, so easy to nick with a careless scrape of the scissor. In fact, the little scissor did brush against the baby's exquisitely fine skin, releasing a drop of blood that drew a scream of horror from her mother.

"They give me the hardest job," Alcira protested. "They want her to hate me from the start!"

And yet Natalia never hated her grandmother.

Grandpa León, always so affectionate and perhaps a little more disheveled, scruffier, always poorly shaved and with red-rimmed eyes, had permission to hold Natalia only when he was sitting down.

Was that what it was like to have children? To be terrified, night and day, of losing them? Esmé didn't want anyone else to touch her baby. Only grudgingly did she allow her husband, her mother, to hold her, but when her in-laws and a few of Guido's siblings, who had stopped by to see them when they came to the capital, and especially their kids, Natalia's little cousins, went over to the crib, she jumped up with a start and stood there, controlling the operation of touching or stroking the baby with the pained impotence of someone who can't stop a harmful action from occurring. Very few dared to pick her up, and when they did, the mother immediately asked them in a quavery voice, imploring, to hand her over, to give her back to her, as if she were afraid of a sudden kidnapping, as if she were begging a dangerous criminal to return a stolen object.

Natalia was six months old when Esmé first agreed to be apart from her for a while and left her in her parents' care, feeling as if her body were being ripped apart. Alcira and León took her for a car ride. When they returned half an hour later, Esmé was standing at the door to her building, her face distorted in a rictus of fear and despair.

A baby was something so exhaustingly fragile. A vast bibliography confirmed it. Accidents, Esmé read, are the leading cause of death for young children. A baby could fall off a bed if it wasn't protected with a barricade of pillows, but it could also be suffocated by those pillows, even by the mattress, if it was too soft (this very uncommon accident was verified by certain statistics); it could die of cold if it wasn't bundled up, but it could also be asphyxiated by its own blanket; it could get hurt without soft crib bumpers; it could drown in its own vomit; it could fall (and, in effect, Natalia once fell from the changing table, at the wriggly age of six months); drown in the bathtub; sustain a burn from an overly warm bottle, and as time went by her fears didn't diminish. Quite the contrary, as Natalia began to move on her own, the fear expanded infinitely: now she might burn herself in the kitchen; she might cut herself with a knife, a pair of scissors, a sheet of paper, on some sharp edge (the whole world had sharp edges); she might stick herself with a nail, a fork, a screw, a pencil, a needle; she might poke any of these things in her eye, into one of her gorgeous, enormous, honey-colored eyes; she might insert her little fingers into an electrical outlet, which in those days were wide enough to admit a baby's finger; she might pull a chair, a cup, a pot, a frying pan filled with hot oil, on top of herself; she might strangle herself with her bib, with the little chain on the pacifier; trap her finger in a door, bang her head against a baseboard, against a piece of furniture, against a wall; choke on a pit, a pebble, a cookie, a button, a coin, a toy, a peanut, a plastic bag; she might plug up her nose with the cap of a ballpoint pen, the eye of a poorly constructed doll; she might swallow a pin, a marble, a crayon, some poison – poison! Everything around her was poison, the world itself was poison: bleach, detergent, the whole gamut of cleaning products, newspaper, soap, medications, batteries, cosmetics, the objects she picked up from the dirty floor, but also food, even food could give her an allergic reaction; her baby might die from inflammation of the glottis every time she ingested a new food. Esmé began by rubbing a little on her skin, and then she added it gradually to familiar foods in minuscule quantities, which she increased with infinite care. Esmé put rubber corner protectors on the low table; she avoided long tablecloths that Natalia might tug on, tipping the dishes on top of herself. She covered the outlets, installed circuit breakers, and put protectors on the doors so that they wouldn't slam shut. At 220 volts, all electrical appliances were a danger. The whole house was dangerous and the outside was dangerous. The sun was dangerous, using public transportation was dangerous, but so was traveling by car. Being pushed down the street in her baby carriage was dangerous: that was the exact height at which car exhaust fumes poisoned the air. And the danger of contagion! Friends, relatives walked in off the street and tried to touch the baby without washing their hands, without rubbing them with alcohol, with disinfectant. The sidewalks were so dirty; people irresponsibly breathed that pestilent, bacteria-infested air on her. People coughed, talked, smoked, expelled their miasma in the same environment that contained her little daughter, polluting the air.

Natalia was an extraordinary miracle in her mother's family and just one more among the youthful rabble of her father's. Those kids, the cousins, so neglected and so many of them, might have colds, fever, bronchitis, flu, chicken pox, tonsillitis, scarlet fever, or one of those nameless rashes, identified only by their number, seventh, eighth, and it was worse, much worse, if those kids appeared to be healthy, because then they might be in the dangerous stage preceding visible symptoms, they might be incubating the disease, the most contagious stage of all.

Esmé felt, or thought she felt, total empathy for her daughter. When they gave Natalia her first injected vaccination, Esmé writhed in pain and threw up when she got home. She had to clench her teeth to keep from screaming when the pediatrician examined her and Natalia cried testily. When she had bronchitis, Esmé didn't sleep for three days, feeling like she herself was choking on the phlegm that interfered with her daughter's breathing. The kinesiologist taught her how to slap her on the back with her cupped hand. One of her hands spanned the baby's entire back, and she had to force herself to slap her in order to help her expel the phlegm – slap her! It was inhumane. It was a miracle that the baby didn't cry when she hit her; it was just additional evidence of that wonder that had arisen from her insides.

Guido, as the child of a large family, was a father in a much more natural way. He knew that babies belong more to their mothers; he took things calmly, with a serene, constant sort of love, less desperate than Esmé's, and, befitting his personality, much more theoretical. As though he had never seen a baby in his life, as though he didn't have one right before his eyes, he avidly read as many books about child development as fell into his hands, and he always had well-founded advice at his fingertips, documented by authorities, on how to educate, feed, or protect Natalia.

When the little girl turned three, aware that her behavior went beyond the norm, even considering that it was a first child, even with an indisputably only child, Esmé decided to go back to work half-days and sent Natalia to preschool.

The day they finished their *adaptation*, the time considered necessary in Argentina for children to get used to preschool and accept separation from their mothers, and which in other, less "psych-crazy" countries simply doesn't exist, Esmé went off to work with chest spasms caused by her repressed sobs. Natalia played calmly and happily in the sandbox, hardly giving her a backward glance and with very little interest when she said goodbye. She seemed almost relieved.

JOURNAL ENTRY 11

I'm writing this journal at the same time as the first draft of the novel. I know that the text, the central story, is going to change quite a bit. What, then, will happen to these commentaries? Will they have meaning in spite of everything? Will I rewrite them, adapting them to the final version? My readers will never know. As they don't yet know the novel's orientation, where its goal lies, which way it's going (unless they've read the back cover, sometimes so dangerously revealing). Everything is a lie, everything is fiction, even this apparent frankness, this disclosure of certain secrets, literary secrets both true and false. I already know many of the situations my characters will have to face. I've jotted them down in a folder labeled "Ideas." Not only that: I also know many things about their destinies, about the general direction of their lives. But I can't tell. All will be revealed at the proper time.

PRESCHOOL AND TURTLE

Could that have been the beginning? Was it that episode in preschool? Her reaction to that episode? Esmé will wonder many years later. Should she have been stricter with her, had a serious conversation, punished her? How do you punish a four-year-old girl? No more candy for a week, two weeks, till the end of the year? Deprive her of her cartoon hour in front of the TV? Though it seems unimaginable today, there was no cable TV in the mid-eighties, just regular channels and a handful of children's shows that all the kids watched at the same time and talked about with one another. Should she have punished her, or just the opposite? Shouldn't she have protected her, immediately taken her out of that place she had chosen for her so carefully, with so much love and fear and apprehension, qualities that, in those days, were nearly the same thing? Shouldn't she have rescued her? Was it good, was it the right decision, to leave her there, in the hands of that too-young, too preoccupied, too "psychological" teacher, that teacher who pre-judged her daughter, and who no doubt didn't treat her like the other kids, who in some way mistreated her?

Esmé walked into the preschool, annoyed at being summoned during working hours yet again. One day was devoted to joining the kids for Cuddly Duck's visit, another to helping them make paper costumes, another to talking to them about her job, which kids that age couldn't understand anyway.

"If I had nothing else to do," Esmé remarked to the other, equally annoyed, moms, "the first thing I'd do would be to pull her out of preschool."

But it was a lie, of course, because like everyone else, Esmé wanted her child to be exactly like the others, like any kid her age and of her social class, and that included a good, expensive preschool.

Despite her annoyance, when she walked into the preschool, she felt with relief that she had left the commotion of the city outside and entered a miniature paradise. She was reassured to see the large sandbox again, which had been so important in influencing her decision. A very difficult decision: Guido and Esmé had visited ten different preschools before determining which was most suitable. Papelito's reputation, the fact that all the dangerous equipment was sitting on sand (there were other preschools where the slide, the seesaw, the climbing bars – which to Esmé were nothing but lethal traps designed to injure or kill her daughter – had been thoughtlessly placed on the hard tiles of the patio), the wonderful detail that the concrete rim containing the sand was protected by pieces of rubber tire, the smiles of the young teachers, with their fair complexions and progressive ideas, who earned a little more than at other institutions, the practical wisdom and experience of the principal, and above all, the other mommies' recommendations, all that had helped her make the difficult decision to earmark a sum for Natalia's preschool that would have sufficed for a down payment on an apartment, including the entire property if you added up all the payments throughout the years.

The appointment was scheduled for after-school hours, and the children, in their pink-and-white (girls) or blue-and-white (boys) checkered smocks, were no longer there, but everything in the little yellow room evoked their presence. The low, brightly-colored chairs, the little work tables, the toys carefully piled up in boxes, *stored and put away/until another day/if we store and put away/ soon we all will play*, and how many times had Esmé tried, fruitlessly, to bring about the song's marvelous effect at home, in Natalia's room.

The teacher was sitting behind a small, portable Formica desk, designed for conversations with parents. She was a young woman with very short hair and a sweet, almost saccharine, smile. To one side, on a wall, were the hooks where the children hung their little bags. Natalia's bore her name and a giraffe that Esmé had embroidered, clumsily, but with her own hands.

"Natalia is fantastic," the preschool teacher started out, predictably.

And she went on to enumerate Natalia's many extraordinary qualities, among which her great intelligence and good social development stood out, especially the influence she had over her peers. Esmé listened, enraptured, her schedule forgotten: she could have stayed there for hours, immersed in the pleasure brought to her by this praise of her daughter. Apparently Natalia possessed leadership qualities, and it was very important to give her guidance at this stage of her life when she could assume that leadership role in a positive way if her parents …

If her parents. Esmé looked at the teacher anxiously. What else did they want of her parents. She sighed, depleted.

"I don't know if you've heard what happened this morning with the turtle, Esmeralda."

Why was this teacher, so much younger than she, addressing her by her first name? It was hard for Esmé to get used to these social changes that were ever more rapidly dismantling the hierarchies she had painstakingly and diligently learned to respect during her childhood in the fifties.

"Yes, Natalia told me. It was that problem boy, right? The same one who gave another little girl a bump on the forehead with the xylophone hammer."

"The turtle incident was terrible for all the children," said the teacher, lowering her gaze, as if the memory of the scene bothered her so much that she could no longer look Esmé in the eye. "We found him floating belly-up in the finger paint bucket."

"How awful!" Esmé agreed, prepared to accompany the teacher in her grief. Now that the conversation had taken a different turn, she was much less interested. She glanced furtively at the clock. In an hour she had a meeting, supposedly informal, but in fact very important, with the owner of the agency and a new client.

"We thought that … Well, Tavito *is* a problem, of course. We're even thinking of asking his parents to withdraw him. Even though he's the right age, he may not be mature enough yet for preschool. And he's about to have a little brother; you know how they get."

But Esmé didn't know, and she never would. She looked at the clock again, this time without trying to hide anything.

"We thought that … It's not only Tavito," the teacher continued. That's what I was trying to tell you when we were talking about leadership. Natalia has a lot of influence on Tavito."

"I'm surprised. She only mentions him to me when she wants to tell me about the trouble he makes. I got the impression he's a pretty wild kid."

"Yes, there's no doubt that Tavito has problems, but … We think it was Natalia who gave him the idea of putting the turtle in the paint bucket."

What nonsense was she talking about? Esmé felt herself shake with indignation, but she contained herself. She immediately caught on to the ridiculous nuances of the situation and responded with a complicit smile.

"Do you mean to tell me that Natalia is accused of being the intellectual author of the Horrific Turtle Murder?"

The preschool teacher appeared to be totally immune to humor or irony.

"The turtle didn't die," she said severely. "But he's at the pet clinic in very serious condition."

JOURNAL ENTRY 12

Materials: I've always been tremendously curious about how and where writers find the materials with which they construct their works. It's strange that, despite being a member of the profession, I continue to be such a naïve reader. I should give myself a hard intellectual bop on the head to make me stop believing that everything the author relates about his characters has actually happened to him. When I read *The World According to Garp*, I was convinced that John Irving had been an only child. From *The Hotel New Hampshire*, it became clear to me that he had been part of a large family. Today it's much easier to consult a biography, but the ingenuous reader doesn't care, or doesn't trust it; he prefers the version that seems most obvious and revels in it. How well does one have to know a reality in order to write about it? They say that Henry James needed only half an hour of peering through the keyhole of a room where a lady was lodging to write the novel *Portrait of a Lady*. I doubt it, but the idea tormented me for a long time.

Materials: the sandbox is the same as the one at Rainbow, the pre-school my three daughters attended. Tavito, the problem child (God knows what his name really was, though even if I did know, I wouldn't tell), was a classmate of one of them in the three-year-olds' group. He hit, bit, and pulled hair. He struck my daughter Paloma on the forehead with the xylophone hammer, raising a slight bump that the teacher decided to remedy in an unforgettable way, by rubbing it with butter. Among the mothers it was rumored that Tavito was beaten quite often at home. The boy also plunged the turtle into the bucket of water that they used for washing their hands after finger painting, but the animal was rescued right away.

In a private school, students are also customers. It must hurt to lose a single one, but it's even more painful when parents start withdrawing the rest of the children. The inspiration for my Tavito was expelled pleasantly, by telling the parents that he wasn't yet mature enough for preschool and, predictably, recommending psychological treatment.

THE DEAD KID

Raised among adults like any oldest child, Natalia complemented her beauty (dark, thick hair, honey-colored eyes, a destructive smile that contained all the grace of the universe) with the advantage of a broad, comprehensive vocabulary, sprinkled with rhetorical flourishes she borrowed from adults. She was quite conscious of the effect it produced and enjoyed startling her teachers.

One Saturday, the day she usually had lunch with her maternal grandparents, she made the whole family laugh and cry at once. Guido couldn't find the salt shaker.

"Where is it?" he asked? "The salt shaker has disappeared!"

"The military took it away," Natalia suddenly exclaimed.

And only then did they realize how, unwittingly, unthinkingly, they were transmitting the story of their lives to the little girl. Grandpa León got up from the table, convulsed with sobs.

Grandma Alcira regaled her with gifts. Natalia had the entire collection of My Little Pony dolls, ridiculously expensive; in her room she had her own little play house, complete with plastic walls and a tiny table and chairs; she owned video cassettes of all her favorite movies, the most complete and complex Playmobil sets, the first Nintendos, and, when the time came, an Atari, the precursor of Play Station.

"Don't you think you're bribing her?" Esmé protested one day, as concerned for her daughter's fragile psyche as for her body, which she continued to think of as eternally endangered. "Aren't you afraid she just loves you out of self-interest?"

"Self-interest is a very good reason to love," replied Alcira. "Why do children love their parents? Because they need them. She doesn't need me, so that's why I have to buy her affection. Like any grandma!"

The little girl got along very well with her granny; however, she rejected Grandpa León, which wasn't hard to understand. Grandpa gave off that sweetish, fruity odor, typical of diabetics who don't take good care of themselves. He had grown slow and heavy and pursued his granddaughter in a touching, but annoying, way, always seeking a kiss on his flabby cheek, a kiss Natalia grudgingly delivered. Esmé tried to transmit to her daughter the love she felt for her dad. She tried to make her know, somehow, the father she had had in her childhood and adolescence. She showed her pictures of a tall, proud man with a blond beard, playing tennis; she told her about her daddy's sense of humor, how he had always cracked jokes; she told her how he helped them put on their "gravely injured" costumes at Carnival to frighten people, and how they all had invented practical jokes for the Day of the Holy Innocents. But that innocence had been lost forever, the Day of the Holy Innocents was no longer celebrated, and the image of the father that Esmé wanted to engrave in her daughter's mind appeared to have no correlation to the real, present, and pathetic figure of Grandpa León.

Esmé regarded Natalia's school notebooks and folders with the trembling, happy passion she once reserved for love letters. Her tidy handwriting, her orderly arithmetic columns, the explosion of light and color in her drawings seemed like an undeserved, glorious miracle. Ever since the dictatorship took over, state education had begun to decline in the country. Natalia attended a private elementary school, which caused her parents, who, like nearly all their generation, had been educated in public schools, some degree of embarrassment. The owner and principal always talked to them about Natalia's great intelligence, and they listened: rapt, innocent customers.

When Natalia was in second grade, while waiting at the schoolhouse door, Esmé met the mother of a new student who had transferred from a different school.

"My son is having a hard time," she said. "I wonder if I did the right thing by changing schools. At the other school he had a lot of friends. But the instruction here is so much better!"

Esmé learned from the other mothers that the new little classmate had a serious degenerative, genetic illness, and that the doctors predicted he wouldn't survive much past adolescence. Esmé thought the woman was crazy; subjecting the child to a change of school was an act of madness. But isn't being a mother a kind of madness? She imagined herself in that mother's place, denying the death sentence in every way possible, trying to act as though her son had a future, as if forgetting about the horror could undo it.

When she ran into her again, she found herself the object of an unexpected request.

"You've got to to help me," the woman said. "My son's classmates have declared war on him, and it seems Natalia is the one in charge of the group."

"They're seven years old," Esmé said. And she remembered the turtle incident. "Children are cruel. The new one always has to pay his dues. I'm sure Natalia doesn't know that your son is sick."

The woman was dressed in jeans, with uncombed hair and an exhausted-looking face.

"They call him the dead kid," she replied.

That afternoon, at milk and cartoon time, Esmé turned off the TV and stood in front of it. It was a sign that they had something very serious to discuss. Natalia looked into her eyes with her confident, frank, and open expression as Esmé spoke to her of the new classmate.

"You guys have to be nice to him. You can't be mean."

"But we're not mean to him," Natalia replied. "He's dumb. He's bad. He stole Florencia's pencil case."

Esmé though that illness and misfortune don't always make people better, nicer, or more generous. Or more intelligent. At seven it's very hard to feel empathy for someone who's suffering so much. It was only logical that the other kids kept their distance.

That night Guido intervened. In his sternest, most persuasive voice, he explained to Natalia why she had to behave especially nicely to the new child. Her honey-colored eyes grew damp, and through her tears, Natalia flashed a smile that brought her parents a stab of love, and, in a way, of relief.

"Now I understand," Natalia said. "I promise we'll never call him the dead kid again."

And she kept her promise. The dead kid's mother thanked Esmé profusely for her intervention. After a birthday party, the dead kid (Esmé hated herself for referring to him like that, even if only to herself, but she couldn't avoid it: she always forgot his name) was admitted to the hospital and missed school for two weeks. There was a rumor among the mothers that at the party a group of children had locked him in a bathroom that had been sprayed with insecticide.

Natalia began coming home with new school supplies, very smart and attractive: an imported pencil case, a metal pencil sharpener in the shape of a helicopter, a brand-name pen that elementary school kids didn't normally use.

"Is it true that your son gives her those things?" Esmé asked the dead kid's mother.

"It's true. Julián is so grateful! It seems that now Natalia is defending him to the group."

Esmé didn't like what was going on, but there wasn't much time to react, because the sick boy was withdrawn from class before the end of the year. By the time she and Guido had talked things over and decided that Naty needed to return everything she had been given, the dead kid had already gone back to his previous school.

JOURNAL ENTRY 13

Taken from real life, of course. A terrible story. In one of my daughters' elementary school classes there was a little boy with a degenerative neurological disease. The mother had transferred him from another school for instructional reasons and it didn't take long for her to regret her decision. The boy often missed school because of his illness; he missed his friends; his new classmates didn't like him and made fun of his problems with the absolute lack of compassion or empathy of seven-year-olds. The following year he returned to his old school. A few years later I learned he had died.

In an earlier version of this journal, I wrote:

> At this point, I have no more excuses. It's a matter of moving forward with the novel's central theme, and that may be impossible. The reader may have begun to suspect that, but I know it. I have three daughters. What follows, what needs to follow according to my plans, is intolerable; it's intolerable to me, and most likely I won't be able to do it.

However, at this point the reader already knows, for physical reasons (the number of pages remaining), that the novel will continue. Therefore, let this comment serve as a reminder that, in the writing of this book, any literary difficulties are compounded by psychological difficulties on the part of the author.

CECILIA

Esmé continued to advance in her career as a copywriter. The nature of her work had changed a great deal since the early seventies, before her time in France, when she had begun working in advertising agencies. In those days, except for certain top-tier agencies, the art department was separate from the copy room. In the art room the radio was always playing, and the writers visited the designers and art directors, who were always ready to chat, even though their hands might have been busily engaged on the production tables, cutting and pasting photolitho copies: that was how the ads were put together, in an artisanal way. When she returned from France, Esmé had to learn to work as part of a team, with an art director, and she discovered how much more sensible and pleasant is was to collaborate in that way. The art folks saw things differently: they fired off images that in turn sparked ideas; they found a system to unify the different ads in a campaign, beginning with a graphic concept, and they were geniuses at fleshing out the commercials that Esmé, who came from the world of words, saw only as empty structures, a mysterious *idea*. She thoroughly enjoyed working à duo beside the tables where the sketches came to life and which were now starting to be replaced by computers.

Now she was the creative director at a medium-sized agency. She earned plenty of money, but she had no fixed schedule: at any moment a lunch, or worse yet, a working dinner, would come up; if it became necessary to stay all night in order to make a presentation on time, Esmé had to be there, coordinating and encouraging her teams. Though she didn't want to think about it, she knew that copywriters' lives are very short. Advertising demands youth; it demands a mindset immersed in the present. Reality, life, the world that you think of as your own, lasts till around forty. It's possible to adapt after that, but it's always tough; you start to look at young people with mistrust, with disapproval, or at the very least, with envy. You start to use that horrible expression "in my day," and the world becomes harder and harder to understand. After that, in the best case scenario, there comes an age of power, but not of creativity, and the only copywriters over fifty that are still going strong are those who have managed to climb the ladder to managerial positions, those who set up their own agencies, those who are able to sell someone else's idea, seducing clients like a snake charmer (because the capacity for seduction knows no age), or those who have become partners in the agency where they were working (and to achieve that, they really do have to be snake charmers).

Whenever someone congratulated Esmé on her professional growth, she couldn't help but think of Cecilia.

Cecilia was from Paraguay, and she was wonderful. She was fat and happy and took care of everything. She wasn't a *live in* because she was married and had a daughter much older than Natalia, who babysat when Guido and Esmé wanted to go out. The interesting professional development of middle-class women in the country depended in good measure on the work of those women, who cleaned other people's houses, took care of other people's children, prepared meals for other families, and had worked outside their own homes since the beginning of time, traveling back and forth from their workplaces, women whom no one ever admiringly asked how they managed to hold down a job and at the same time look after their own houses, their husbands, and their kids.

Only to Cecilia could Esmé entrust her daughter in that way. Ever since she had gone back to work in advertising, a single, hideous fantasy came to replace and consolidate the compendium of fears that had driven her crazy when her daughter was a baby. Esmé feared that Natalia would fall out the window. The balcony of the house had a very tall, vine-covered security railing. But there were no bars on the windows. Esmé hadn't been able to convince Guido of that necessity; he called her crazy, and most likely he was right. In a recurrent dream that made her wake up screaming, she came home from work and found herself among a very large group of people that included her neighbors, but sometimes also her parents, her cousins, or her colleagues, all gathered at the entrance to her building, surrounding something that couldn't be seen. They didn't look at her or speak to her. Esmé elbowed her way through the crowd because they wouldn't let her pass, though they didn't push her away, either. At last she managed to catch a glimpse of whatever it was that they were all looking at so intently and so silently: in the midst of the crowd, lying on the ground, there was a smashed pumpkin, and that pumpkin was her daughter.

And so every time Esmé returned home, a hand-shaped angst squeezed her heart as she approached the building, and she began to breathe again when she saw that there was no unusual group of people gathered in the doorway, when she walked down the hall to take the elevator and the super greeted her normally, with a smile. Then she regained her composure and opened the door to her apartment, knowing that nothing had happened, that one more day had gone by without her daughter having fallen out the window, and that was thanks to Cecilia, the one and only, the fat, wonderful Cecilia. Even though they had known one another for years, Esmé addressed her with the formal *usted*, as a sign of respect and affection. And Cecilia, more informally, called her *vos*, because that's how Paraguayan women talked.

Of course, it was a complex relationship. Esmé both loved and hated Cecilia, because she relied on her and because Cecilia spent many more hours a day with her daughter than she herself did. Naty adored her. And Cecilia, like any domestic worker (words like "servant" and "girl" were no longer used, and "cleaning woman" was inadequate to describe someone so powerful), both loved and hated her boss, because she had to wash her clothes and make her meals and take care of her daughter and clean her filth and that of her family, because Esmé had everything she didn't and because she had enough left over to pay Cecilia's salary. Although, in Ceci's case, you had to be keenly aware of the situation to imagine that hatred, which the woman concealed even to herself. Guido didn't understand or care about the complexity of the situation: for him Cecilia was a terrific fat lady who brewed him the best *mates*.

The "terrific fat lady" designation wouldn't have gone down at all well with Cecilia, who was desperate to lose weight and attended Obesity Anonymous meetings. She didn't eat any of what she prepared for other people in their homes and wasn't tempted by cookies or bread. Instead she brought along plastic containers with the scant, light meals permitted by her diet, consisting mostly of vegetables. In the fridge there was always a large soda bottle that Cecilia filled with a liquid resembling fruit juice, nearly calorie-free, and which she drank all day long to control her appetite, with limited success, since whenever she managed to lose seven or eight pounds, she gained them right back again.

One fatal, accursed day, Esmé began to notice that money was missing from the bedroom drawer where she kept what she called her "petty cash box." Neither she nor Guido was overly cautious, and from that moment on, they resolved to count the money together every night. It soon became all too obvious that someone was taking out money in a regular, foreseeable way.

"Cecilia," said Guido.

"Impossible," said Esmé.

They really hadn't wanted to mention it to Natalia, but suddenly, in the middle of their discussion, there she was, looking at them, flustered. She looked very flushed.

"What's wrong, Naty?" Esmé asked.

"I saw it … I saw her," Natalia said.

"What did you see? Who?"

"Cecilia. I saw Cecilia taking money out of the drawer. But she made me promise I'd never tell you. She said that if I told you, she'd be very angry with me. And she would hit me."

Hit her! Esmé felt her knees buckle. She had been leaving her daughter alone for hours with a person who threatened to hit her. Who possibly *did* hit her! What kind of rotten, monstrous mother was she to do that to her own daughter? Then she shook her head. When it comes to human conduct, nothing is impossible, but it was hard for her to think of Cecilia as capable of hitting Natalia, who, besides, was a big enough girl to defend herself when talking to her parents.

"Did she ever hit you?" asked Guido in such an indignant, threatening voice, that Natalia recoiled.

"No, Papito, Cecilia never, ever hit me. That's why I didn't believe her ... Cecilia is nice. But then she said that if I didn't tell, she would pick up my room every afternoon before Mamá gets home."

That seemed more likely. Esmé believed that a nine-year-old girl should be able to keep her room reasonably neat, and she waged an intense, constant war to achieve that outcome. She had asked Cecilia not to get involved, and the last few times it seemed to her that she was making progress.

"Tomorrow I'll talk to her," she said to Guido, with an unhappy sigh. "I don't have the heart to accuse her of anything. I'll tell her that ... I don't know. I'll think of some excuse."

Esmé knew that Cecilia had money problems. Her husband had fallen and broken his arm while fixing the roof of their house. The man did odd jobs, and in his present condition he couldn't work; all the weight of keeping up with the house fell to Cecilia. Esmé had given her a loan, which she was expected to repay gradually out of her salary.

Their conversation the following day was painful. Guido and Esmé had decided to fire her, but they would forgive the loan and give her a lump sum of severance pay.

"I know what you're accusing me of," Cecilia said when she learned they were about to fire her. "And I'm telling you you're wrong."

"But Cecilia, I'm not accusing you of anything," Esmé said. "It's just that I've decided to spend less time at work and concentrate more on the house."

"Don't lie to me, Esmeralda, I know you have money missing." Cecilia's voice broke in a sob and she lowered her head. "But I swear to you by everything that's holy that you're wrong." And she kissed the medal of the Virgin that she always wore around her neck.

Cecilia took the Tupperware container with her food and the bottle of juice out of the refrigerator. She asked for permission to stop by and visit Natalia once in a while, but she never showed up again. In time Esmé discovered that one year after leaving her house, Cecilia had fallen victim to an inexplicable, raging bout of psychosis, quite rare at her age (she was forty-two) and was hospitalized at the Moyano Clinic.

One day she ran across her in the street, practically in rags, carrying a large, worn-out bag. By then the entire episode had taken on a different meaning in her memory. She embraced her warmly.

"Cecilia! It's me, Esmé!"

"I saw you. I may be crazy, but I'm not blind," Cecilia said. "Do you have a cigarette?"

"You know I don't smoke, Ceci."

Cecilia studied her with that sly gaze crazy people acquire when they've been locked up for a long time and no longer expect anything good from the world.

"Then give me money to buy some."

.

JOURNAL ENTRY 14

Although there are many discrepancies, Cecilia is modeled on Mary, a woman who worked at my house for many years when my daughters were small. We were very fond of one another and called each other by the formal *usted* (she wasn't Paraguayan). Her three daughters were older than mine and at some point worked for me as babysitters. Mary was fat, and she suffered. She found help through ALCO (Association for the Struggle against Obesity) groups.

Suddenly, just like that, my dear Señora Mary, a person who had been perfectly normal, fell into a very serious depression that changed the expression on her face. Her depression worsened to the point that she had to stop working because she could no longer get out of bed. She was treated with a battery of antidepressants. One day she came over to say hello; she looked like a different person. Her face was twisted, deformed into a grimace, her eyes shining and unfocused. She spoke incoherently, unable to finish a sentence, and she constant resorted to the expressions "you understand" and "you know" to fill in the blanks.

Señora Mary (that was what we always called her) was a sensible, intelligent, even-tempered, cheerful person. My daughters loved her as much as I did. At the age of 39 she went crazy, and nobody could do a thing for her. For a while I followed her through a long, varied series of area psychiatrists. Her husband's benefit society – he was a custodian at a government office – paid for her hospitalizations and medical care, but she didn't have a designated psychiatrist in charge of her case. The doctors, who visited the psychiatric hospitals once in a while, were always seeing her for the first time. Mary went in and out of madhouses, and there was no one to consolidate the records of her illness, no one to talk to, no one to take an interest in her as a person, no one who knew her, no one who could explain what was happening to her or why. I went to visit her with her husband a few times. Sometimes we found her with injuries: we were told that she had fallen down the stairs or had bumped into a door. The medications that controlled her symptoms turned her into a clumsy, indifferent, passive thing that sucked on candies to alleviate her dry mouth, stained at the corners with crusty saliva. When she was off her medicines, she screamed and defended herself against enemies invisible to the rest of us, received messages over the radio and TV, or from posters that appeared in the air; she heard voices that tortured her. There are no words to convey the suffering of her daughters, who at the time were teenagers and didn't want to visit her. They couldn't bear seeing her like that. She never recovered.

GRANDPA LEÓN

The second time Esmé found a condom in Guido's pocket, it came as no surprise. Several years had gone by, and this time it wasn't a package, but just one, carefully encased in its transparent, individual wrapper. Esmé wasn't wearing Guido's jacket, but rather checking its pockets before sending it to the dry cleaner. The function of condoms had changed quite a bit: AIDS had returned them to their original purpose, the one that had lent them their official name, prophylactics: to prevent disease in their users. Detested by the men of his generation, they had, nevertheless, become necessary. And even though men resisted taking those precautions, many women insisted on them.

One night Naty stayed over at a friend's house for a pajama party. And at dinner time Guido found the condom sitting on top of his plate.

"Haha – I'll bet you found it in the blue jacket!"

"Yes," replied Esmé. And she had to explain herself: Could she be one of those women who check their husbands' pockets? "I was going to send it to the dry cleaner."

"Someone gave it to me in the street," said Guido, as quick as usual, but less convincing. "Some kids were handing them out, an AIDS awareness campaign. Don't tell me that never happened to you!"

It was possible, of course, but it wasn't true, and Esmé knew it, and Guido knew that she knew. Without further comment, she accepted the excuse and decided to keep it for the moment in the excuse box, which was already stuffed with unexplained trips, ridiculous working hours, a pair of women's black sunglasses found in the car (they belonged to a client who was never going to pick them up, Guido explained, giving them to Esmé as proof of his innocence), or the attempt to explain away the mascara smear on his shirt as a grease stain from the car. (Had she been crying, the mascara wearer? Had she cried over him?) They both knew that the drawer was filled to overflowing, that there was no room for even one more excuse, and that when they went to open it, they would never be able to close it again.

Why didn't Esmeralda insist? Why didn't she forge ahead, mentioning schedules and attitudes and those phone calls that went dead as soon as the caller heard her voice? Could she be one of those women who would rather not face the truth, who are afraid? Of course not. Esmé was capable of imagining the worst and meeting it head on. She was a strong, direct, independent woman, and she was not afraid. She could live perfectly well without Guido. There were other reasons, which at the moment, as they ate in silence, without looking at one another (the TV helped), she couldn't quite recall. Reasons for not continuing to dig in that ground where the dirt had been stirred up, where it was obvious that something was buried, and not exactly hidden treasure, either. Guido's voice, for example, his tone, which changed so drastically without his realizing it when he sometimes answered the phone And those damned words, "Same here," which he uttered in a ridiculously impersonal way. Same here, ditto, the most appropriately formal, distant reply under the circumstances to an "I love you," the reply that avoided the dangerous "Me too." No, Esmé wasn't afraid. Not one bit. Or maybe just a little.

A few days later Esmé went out shopping with her mother. Naty, who at the time still hated display windows, mall strolling, and fitting rooms, stayed behind at her grandparents' house watching TV, in León's care. Like any intelligent woman, Alcira knew that one of the wisest axioms in the language was the one that said that outsiders should mind their own business, but in everything having to do with her daughter's marriage, she took Guido's part, or perhaps the part of the institution itself. She knew that neither the advice nor remarks of others held sway over a couple's always mysterious intimacy. If the marriage was falling apart anyway, at least no one would be able to accuse her of helping to unleash the catastrophe. If the couple stayed together, her daughter would hate her less when she remembered Alcira's words in her husband's defense. Esmé understood her mother's position all too well, and if she wanted to talk to her, it was precisely for that reason, because she needed to hear intelligent arguments in Guido's favor.

Instead of exploring clothing stores, they sat down in a lovely old, but remodeled, coffee house to have tea with cookies that were like the ones Esmé recalled from her childhood. They spoke for nearly three hours.

When they returned home, the TV was blasting away so loudly that it could be heard from the elevator.

Natalia was sitting calmly in front of the set, and Grandpa León was dead.

They found him in the bedroom, sprawled out on the floor beside the bed. He was wearing the same pajamas he had on when they left him. Lately it had been hard to persuade him to get dressed if he had no need to go outside. The two of them knew immediately that he was dead: by his color, his immobile, yet tense, posture, and by a certain ineffable quality, that murkiness emitted by corpses. The two of them, without needing to consult one another, pretended that the situation was serious, but fixable. They called for an ambulance and covered him with a blue quilt, as if they could shield him from such cold. They tried to keep Natalia in the living room, but they couldn't prevent her frightened little face from peeking in at the bedroom door. Esmé hugged her as if trying to push her back into her own body, to protect her from the horror of life.

The doctor who arrived with the ambulance confirmed what they already knew and refused to take him away. He had been dead for about two hours, they told them. There was no way of being sure without an autopsy, but with his health history, a massive coronary wouldn't be an unusual explanation. The doctor was very young, very dark, and very nervous. He had a slight speech defect that made his words somewhat difficult to understand, especially for Alcira, who was hard of hearing. There wasn't much to say, but the young man was obviously distressed and spoke at length of sympatho-adrenal activation, normal cardiac repolarization, increased thrombogenesis, inflammation, and vasoconstriction, as if those mysterious words, incomprehensible to the layman, were part of a ritual that would somehow help them accept the unacceptable.

Only when the doctor had gone did Alcira finally burst into tears, and Esmé went to call Guido. Naty was very quiet, curled up in a corner of the big armchair.

In the days the followed, Alcira asked many questions. As if knowing, finding out the details, could turn back the clock and right wrongs. Had Grandpa asked for something sweet? Maybe – she wasn't sure, Naty replied. But hadn't she explained to her that Grandpa was diabetic? That sugar was bad for him, very bad? Hadn't there been a Coke in the refrigerator? Alcira asked. There was, Naty explained, and she had drunk it. It was very cold and delicious. Grandpa had been looking for something in the kitchen (sugar, Alcira thought, he was looking for sugar, sugar, sugar; he knew he was having an attack of hypoglycemia and was desperately looking for sugar) and then he went to the bedroom. The sugar bowl, though, was in its usual place. Didn't Grandpa scream? Didn't he ask for help?

"Mamá, are you crazy? Leave her alone. Are you going to accuse a ten-year-old little girl of drinking a Coke?"

"I'm not crazy, she's not so little, and I'm not accusing her of anything. I just want to know."

"To know what? Papá killed himself; you know that. He'd been killing himself slowly, for a long time. Did you want to know more? You could have requested an autopsy!"

"I want to know why, child. Why, when we were together our whole lives long, why the hell wasn't I with him at that moment. That's what I want to know!"

The important thing, the only important thing, was that the guilty feeling, that damned guilt, wouldn't harm Natalia, the last person to see Grandpa alive, the one who was with him when he died.

"Do you miss Grandpa?" Esmé asked her a few days later.

"Sometimes yes and sometimes no." Natalia looked at her with her limpid eyes. "Grandpa smelled bad."

Esmé caressed her, moved by her candor. Life would teach her to lie. Meanwhile, they had to do something to counteract that horrid experience, to free her of the painful guilt of being the last person to see her grandfather alive and being unable to do anything to help him. And so Naty's parents decided to give her the quintessential Argentine cure, the national panacea for all the ills of body and soul.

Natalia began her first treatment with a child psychologist whose office, luckily, was located in the same building where the family lived, one less place to drive her back and forth to. At first Natalia refused to go to the office. She said it was boring, that Dr. Eberman always wanted to play cards, and she always lost. That she only knew how to play rummy and Go Fish. Later she stopped talking about it, and her parents felt relieved when the doctor invited them to her office. They needed information.

After a long, uncomfortable silence, which the therapist considered necessary, the meeting began in a more or less traditional fashion.

"Why do you think I asked you here for a conversation?"

Esmé attempt several responses that dissolved in the silence. Guido just listened. The reason Dr. Eberman finally offered was easy to understand: Naty had missed many appointments and besides, they hadn't yet paid for the first month.

Guido and Esmé looked at one another, befuddled. It took a while for them to realize that Natalia had kept the money, quite a considerable sum. But that aside, where had she been when she told them she was at therapy?

Natalia didn't try to deny anything. With sound arguments, she explained to them that the doctor was a fool (something Guido had already begun to suspect), that there was no mental problem, that at her appointment times she met with her school chums at the new, neighborhood shopping mall, and that she had spent the money on milkshakes and candy. She suggested that, instead of sending her to the psychologist, they might buy her a computer. And then she made her parents' eyes well up with tears.

"I promise I'll pay it all back, to the very last cent."

"With what money, Naty?" Esmé asked, sterner than ever.

"With my tooth money. I still have a few baby teeth left!"

Despite being touched by her offer, Guido and Esmé decided that the tooth fairy would bring Natalia no more money for her teeth, which she would no longer place under her pillow. The mall was off-limits for the rest of the year. Esmé had a meeting with the teacher that ended up reassuring her. There were three clear parameters of normal school behavior: if a child didn't cause disruptions in class, got good grades, and had friends, she was normal. According to the teacher, Natalia was perfectly fine.

Her grandfather's death didn't seem to have fazed her very much, her behavior hadn't changed, and as usual, she had many friends over whom she seemed to exert great influence. They decided to liberate her from Dr. Eberman.

"If we force her, it won't work," Esmé said, abashedly telling her mother the story.

"That girl takes after me!" said Grandma Alcira, laughing. "Haven't I told you a thousand times that I used to keep my piano lesson money and spend it on buying my classmates orange soda and ham-and-cheese sandwiches at the milk bar?"

"Yeah, yeah, you've told me a thousand times! Both me and her! That's where she got the idea!"

"Oh, of course. As usual, now you're going to blame me. All right, I'm your mother – I'm used to it."

The fact was that Natalia's childhood was coming to an end. If you put your ear to the ground, you could already hear the gallop of adolescence approaching, thundering along with its iron hooves.

JOURNAL ENTRY 15

This family still doesn't have a last name. It's no small matter. A surname reveals origins, defines certain customs, a certain type of relationship between the characters, certain family memories. Esmé seems Jewish; it's inevitable. Guido could be of Mediterranean background, though I'd rather not rely on the cliché of the average Argentine family, made up of Spaniards or Italians, or their very frequent mixture. They might also be Croats or Greeks ...

The Web tells me that twenty-one countries form part of the Mediterranean Basin: eleven European nations, five Asian ones, and five African. After all, my own paternal grandmother was of Moroccan origin.

And I'm still uncertain.

A comment about the plot (or lack thereof) of this quasi-novel. I'm not capable of handling a closed story line, and it doesn't interest me much, either. I've never been fascinated by detective novels, and in more general terms, I'm annoyed by those novels where, in the final chapters, some secret is revealed that changes or gives meaning to whatever came before. Over time, and through my readings, I've come to like closed plots less and less; they strike me as increasingly predictable. Even in remarkable novels like *The Sea* or *Ancient Light* by John Banville, I'm irritated by the deliberate concealment of certain facts, designed to surprise the reader, who, thanks to experience, is no longer surprised by anything. On the other hand, I admire those open-plot novels with loose ends, apparently devoid of suspense (thought they do possess it), and especially without intrigue or resolution, like Kawabata's *Beauty and Sadness; The House of the Sleeping Beauties*.

For some reason, I don't feel the need to mention my formative readings in this diary, but rather those books that I'm reading as I write. Perhaps precisely because it's a diary.

DIVORCE

At times Esmé tried to examine her own life from the outside. How, for example, would she tell the story of her marriage? Through their fights? Their happy moments? Through certain daily events? Could she put herself in Guido's place, see herself from his perspective? She couldn't; she didn't want to.

It's a story that could be told through three very similar situations. This scene, the third in which an element found in a pocket plays a role, takes place in a traditional Buenos Aires restaurant. It's very late. Guido and Esmeralda have had dinner with friends. The place evokes memories of their childhoods. From the menu to the slightly moth-eaten deer heads adorning the walls, everything predisposes them to tenderness.

The dinner is over. There are six people around the table. They're drinking coffee and smoking. Smoking in public places hasn't been outlawed yet. Within six years, of the six people sitting at this table, one will have died of cancer (a kind of cancer unrelated to tobacco), and three others will have given up smoking. One of the women takes out a cigarette, and Guido lights it for her with a match, making an amusing remark about the steadfast reliability of matches compared to the best lighter.

Esmé takes the little box of matches that Guido has removed from his pocket and which has an ad for a by-the-hour hotel.

"What's this?" she asks calmly, as if she didn't know.

Then, unexpectedly, especially for herself, Esmé gives her husband a slap, which he returns almost immediately, This is something new, a rapid concurrence of events that had never before taken place between them and that will never happen again. Both of them are astonished at what has just occurred They look at one another, perplexed. How to go on now? What happens next? Their friends, embarrassed, don't know if they should intervene, get up and leave, or pretend that nothing is wrong and keep making conversation.

"What do I have to do?" Esmé asks her mother a few days later, with the intention of doing the exact opposite.

"What do you feel like doing?" Alcira replies, knowing perfectly well what her daughter expects of her and unwilling to give her the satisfaction.

"I don't know. I don't even know if I'm the one who decides. What a son-of-a-bitch."

"And you never …?"

"Don't make comparisons. That has nothing to do with it. Adultery is the least of it. What Guido's doing is carelessness, indifference – it's that nothing about me matters to him. I'm not even important enough to make him throw the matches away instead of sticking them in his pocket!"

By the time Natalia started high school, there had already been a computer in her home for several years, and, like a good portion of her generation, she was the daughter of separated parents.

JOURNAL ENTRY 16

I've been reading the memoir of a man who never was a writer, Emilio Poblet Díaz. Touching precisely because of what it lacks in literary qualities, these recollections tell, among other things, the terrifying story of Emilio's father's madness. Lost in his psychotic nightmare, the man tries to kill his eight-year-old son, who is everything he has in the world.

I'm not going to add anything new to the ancient subject of filicide, extensively studied by psychoanalysts and sociologists. The love of parents for their children is a love that includes a dose of madness. One pinch too many turns into hatred, includes hatred. It isn't just to take revenge on Jason that Medea kills her sons. It's also to free herself of those sons; it's because of the sons themselves, because of the frenzied relationship that binds them, that feeling of absolute dependence provoked by maternal love. We depend on what we love. When we love in such an absolute, brutal way, we depend absolutely, brutally. Who really wants their children to be independent? The only truly independent person is he who loves no one. He who loves, lives the life of the beloved, follows her fortunes. We are revived in a child's smile; we die in that child's tears. How could we possibly not hate them? isn't it natural, then, that a mother, talking about her small children, sometimes says – that traditional, symbolic phrase – *they make me want to throw them off the balcony*? Isn't it natural that sometimes, in a fit of madness, she sometimes does throw them off, and herself along with them? Isn't it natural to want to kill someone we love so much? Why aren't they a part of us? How dare they have their own tastes, desires, illusions, knowledge, hopes, and not ours? It's unacceptable; it's intolerable for them to be people separate from our bodies, from our psyches. "Your children are children of the wind," said Kahlil Gibran, my generation's (second-rate) guru. A ridiculous lie.

Perhaps that's why I feel within me the need for this novel, this daughter. As I write it, I'm reading other books about difficult children, something that seems to be a typical manifestation of the angst of my generation, disturbed because of what came later, the result, perhaps, of our own rebellion. In *What I Loved*, Siri Hustvedt has the good sense to tell the story, not from the perspective of one of the parents, but rather through a family friend. I've just finished Herman Koch's *The Dinner*, a sort of detective novel, which has the unsettling ability to persuade, to have the reader identify with the arguments of an intelligent, sensible person who also happens to be a monster. *The Dinner* includes the brilliant idea of portraying the father as just as horrible and deformed as the son. My Esmé: isn't she too generous, too good, too normal? But, couldn't that be how any mother feels, how she sees herself, despite her guilt?

The Babysitter

"For your sake, I'm not calling the police. And I don't know if I'm doing you a favor," Pilar said.

At 4:30 AM Esmé leaped out of bed, jolted from a peaceful dream by the urgent ringing of the phone. In the few seconds it took her to pick up, she had time to settle her nerves. Natalia hadn't gone out with friends, wasn't out dancing, wasn't camping somewhere. And if she had been, could Esmé have possibly been asleep? And having a peaceful dream?

Natalia was babysitting Pilar's little girl.

It had been Alcira's idea, a good one.

"It's important for her to earn her own money," the grandmother had said. "For her own good, for her pride. And so she'll see that it doesn't always fall from heaven."

The heaven from which money usually fell into Natalia's hands was her grandmother's house. Her grandmother, who no longer gave her sophisticated toys, but money in quantities that were hard to determine.

"I want her to keep visiting her grandma like when she was little," Alcira said, referring to herself in the third person. "And to make that happen, there has to be a good reason. Let her come for the money: I don't care, as long as I see her."

Natalia had lunch at her grandmother's house once a week. How much was Alcira giving her? It was difficult to ask Natalia directly, as she mentioned tiny, unrealistic amounts. Alcira refused to tell.

"It's a secret between us," she said. "But don't worry – it's nothing that will change her life."

And yet Natalia's life *had* changed a great deal, somehow becoming a challenge to finance. How much was Guido giving her? Very little, Esmé thought, as little as what he gave her in support. Or was it just the opposite? Did he give his daughter everything he denied his wife? This was even more difficult to know, because she couldn't ask Natalia directly. These days there wasn't much she could ask her directly. Esmé was quite aware of what it meant to enter adolescence. Her own had possibly been the first generation of kids to become real adolescents, as the word was currently understood. Never before the sixties had there been such an inter-generational rupture. Alcira's stories (and the photos, films, and books) spoke of a different era, perhaps a happy one, when puberty (that period of life, now long-vanished, when kids were acne-ridden, ungainly, and shy, powered by a combination of hormonal awakening and social repression) lasted till age fourteen, and then people turned into young adults. The young adults, anxious to leave childhood, and especially puberty, behind, limited themselves to imitating their elders. Boys put on long pants; girls proudly began wearing their mother's clothing; everyone danced to the same music. Just as things had been since prehistoric times, the old folks grumbled about the young ones, but the leap, the breach, wasn't insurmountable. The decade of the sixties in the twentieth century was perhaps the time when that fissure grew wider and deeper, becoming a moat full of crocodiles whose purpose was to defend the castle of an increasingly defined, more prestigious, and more prolonged adolescence, with its own music, fashions, and language, imitated by children and adults alike.

Esmé hadn't forgotten the passionate arguments she had had with her own parents, especially with Alcira, and she prepared herself for her daughter's criticisms of her life, her clothing, and her friends. In that first stage of adolescence, at least, Naty's reactions caught her by surprise. Natalia was always affectionate, she never confronted her, and on the rare occasions when Esmé got angry at her, she stood up and walked out of the room, discreet and terrible, and there was no stopping her. In her subtle way, without causing a commotion, she too had become an expert in the art of manipulating separated parents.

Mamá, I have a problem, her daughter said over the telephone in the early morning hours, and the wonder of hearing her voice, whole and healthy, returned Esmeralda's soul, which had been fluttering near the ceiling, to her unraveled body. Pilar snatched the phone away from Natalia. She sounded very upset. Esmé got dressed as fast as she could, hopped into her car, and flew over there. She was sorry she had ever suggested that babysitting job. She knew Pilar well and understood that she was capable of spinning out of control in a fit of anger. Now the only important thing was to rescue her daughter. They'd discuss what had happened when they were back home.

This was the third time Natalia had sat for Agustina, Pilar's six-year-old daughter, when her parents went out. The other two occasions had turned out fine, a few hours: a party, a movie date. But this time they had gone to Chascomús to visit Gastón's mother (Pilar's mother-in-law), and they planned to spend the night there. It was a Friday: they had asked Natalia to stay until noon on Saturday.

"We had to come back in the middle of the night! We could have had an accident on the road!"

Pilar was screaming wildly, her face red with outrage. Behind her, Gastón, looking downcast, made signs to Esmé not to answer her. Unnecessary signs, because Esmé knew her friend well enough to understand that nothing would be worse than to throw more wood on the fire when she was in such a state. Better to let her get it off her chest. She had plenty of reasons. The condition of the apartment was remarkable. Esmé had never seen anything like it. Natalia was sitting on a little bench (the defendant's box), and Esmé first thought was that she had never seen her daughter looking so beautiful. Her thick, black hair spilled over the deep neckline of a party dress that Esmé didn't recognize (but who could recognize all Natalia's clothes?), and her honey-colored eyes were delicately made up with liner that was slightly smudged on the lower lids, emphasizing the dark circles that at age fourteen highlighted the still-childlike beauty of her face.

The first thing Esmé noticed as she entered the apartment was how her feet stuck to the parquet floor with each step. A dark, sticky substance covered the entire floor in a relatively even layer. That uniform film was interrupted here and there by pools of vomit, especially in the corners. Later she would discover that the guests who were invited to the impromptu party had stumbled around the house, spilling their beverages (mostly Coke with Fernet) and stepping on the spilled liquid. There were paper cups everywhere, no sign that anything had been eaten, and an astonishing quantity of wine cartons and empty bottles of alcohol of various varieties and sizes. There were glasses filled with ashes and cigarette butts that had also been tossed on the floor and on the table. The cushions, the chairs, a coffee table, and the carpet beneath it revealed wine stains and the occasional burn. Chairs had been turned upside-down, their cushions scattered on the ground, and the two curtains from the balcony windows had been partially pulled off, as if someone had grabbed them in an attempt to keep from falling. Additionally, there was an amazing, inexplicable quantity of hair everywhere, mostly stuck to the floor. Someone had swept pieces of broken glass and bits of china or ceramic against the wall and taken the trouble of getting the rest of the decorations, ashtrays and vases, out of the way, piling them on top of the bookcase.

"How's Agustina?" Esmé asked.

"The child is fine, sleeping peacefully" Gastón said.

"Mamá, mamita," said Natalia, who had perceived the horror, but also the love, in her mother's expression. "We were going to put it all back together. We wanted to clean and straighten up, but they wouldn't let us!"

"Clean and straighten up? And what about everything you broke? And what you destroyed? What were you planning to do about the floor?"

"I don't know, said Natalia, a little disconcerted, eyes lowered … Maybe mop it?"

"You were going to mop the parquet, you miserable wretch! And ruin it altogether! The neighbors called us at two AM! Do you know where we found this little slut? In our bed, screwing with some boy!"

The words "slut" and "screwing" produced a sort of magical effect in Esmé. If until then she had lowered her head, ashamed of Natalia's behavior, now she straightened her spine and looked at her friends with a fury equal to theirs, prepared to fight back. Even though she had just found out, she was very proud of her daughter's sexual freedom. Hadn't she and even Pilar herself rebelled, hadn't they fought, against the sentence that limited and chained women's desire? Hadn't they taken on all the powers of the establishment to gain that freedom that Pilar now insulted with the same words others had hurled at them? Hadn't they used the expression "screwing around" to make them feel they were doing something filthy, forbidden, dirty, which lowered them to a category far below those women who exchanged sex for money?

"I won't let you talk about my daughter in those terms," she said firmly.

But Pilar wasn't looking at her. She was completely beside herself, at a point where her floods of anger overflowed the banks marked by words and spilled into deeds. Esmé had heard stories of how Pilar was capable of destroying a set of dishes by methodically smashing one piece after another on the floor, or shredding her husband's best suits with a scissor. All of a sudden, Pilar hurled herself against Natalia, panting fiercely. She grabbed her by her clothes and started shaking her, all the while insulting her with the most diverse vocabulary the language allowed. Natalia didn't try to defend herself; she merely looked at her with wide eyes and a half-smile that seemed to infuriate the owner of the house even more. Gastón and Esmé had to intervene and separate them.

"Pilar, honey, come here," Gastón beckoned, holding her arms and trying to bring her back from that distant, alien place that was her unleashed fury. "Come with me, let's go to the kitchen and I'll make you some tea. You'll take a Riotril and go right to bed, and I'll clean …"

And meanwhile he gestured to Esmé and Natalia to go away.

"I'll pay for everything," Esmé said before she left.

"Of course you'll pay for everything! Because I'm not gonna bother to sue you in court! I'm gonna go to your house and smash up everything – I'll leave it like you left mine!" Pilar shouted, while her husband pushed her gradually toward the kitchen, whispering softly into her ear, like people do with horses.

In the car Esmé didn't know what to say.

"You never told me you had a boyfriend."

"I don't Mamá. I would have told you. You would have been the first to know." Natalia looked and her with her trusting, calm face.

"Pilar lied?"

"No, she didn't lie. But he wasn't a boyfriend. He was just a boy. Didn't you ever do something with a boy who wasn't your boyfriend?"

On reflection, Esmé had to admit that yes, she had. That no matter how much her mother had tried to instill the idea that a woman only feels sexual desire for the man she loves, Esmé, guilty and perturbed, had been turned on more than once by men she didn't love at all. Although not at Natalia's age, of course. Or had she? Memory is so precarious …

"*Hijita*, there's just one thing that …"

"You've told me so many times, Mamá. Don't worry – yes, only with a condom. Always, always, always. I'm not suicidal. I don't want to get pregnant, and I don't want to die of AIDS."

"Where did all that hair come from?" she asked, in part to keep the conversation going somehow, and also out of sheer curiosity.

"A boy fell asleep in a chair and two others decided to play a joke on him, and so they cut his hair."

Esmé sighed, as her mind plodded ahead, trying to organize a plan of action. She would have to talk to Guido, to tell him everything. There would have to be a long serious talk with Natalia, with both parents together. It was important to show a united front in situations like this. Obviously Esmé would pay for the cleaning and repairs out of her current and future savings. They would have to come up with some sort of punishment. How do you punish a fourteen-year-old girl? There aren't many possibilities other than to ground her. She wouldn't say a word to her mother. Why reveal another example of her failure. Then she asked Natalia the only thing that still remained an inexplicable mystery.

"How is it possible that Agustina didn't wake up? With all that music? And then with Pilar's screaming?"

"She's six, Mamá. Agustina always sleeps well. Don't you know that little kids sleep very soundly? She was still up when the first kids arrived. Maybe she drank something from a glass; it's impossible to be everywhere."

154

And after an oppressive silence, Natalia's little voice was heard once more:

"Mamita … forgive me. It was a disaster. I deserve all the blame. Go ahead and punish me. I'll pay with my savings. I couldn't stop it, you know? It was Rita. She didn't let me know. We had arranged for her to come and visit me that night, and I gave her Pilar's address. I never thought she would invite everyone to a party. It was terrible. Lots of people showed up that I didn't even know, with drinks … I swear I tried to throw them out, but they kept on coming … It got out of control …"

Although his partner referred to their joint enterprise as "the little workshop," Guido insisted on calling it "the textile business," and he was always very busy with his work as a businessman, which included reading books on economics and biographies of outstanding entrepreneurs. He grudgingly accepted the unhappy task of getting angry at his daughter.

"Didn't you know your friend Pilar? You know she's a nut job!" he said to Esmé. "You made a big mistake sticking poor Naty in that house. Just the same, I'll talk to your daughter. This time she went too far."

One week later, when Pilar called to say that she had noticed that a package of dollars was missing from a drawer, Esmé detected a quiver of hesitation in her former friend's voice and didn't even bother asking Natalia.

"That Naty is something else!" Alcira said to her, sometime later. "Your daughter has business genes, like her dad and her grandfather. She told me how she organized a party, collecting admission fees, and that it turned out very well."

But without a doubt, Esmé thought, feeling a little guilty because merely thinking about it implied a degree of doubt, a secret accusation against her daughter, without a doubt it wasn't the same party.

JOURNAL ENTRY 17

Another novel about a difficult child: *We Need to Talk about Kevin.* In fiction bad children tend to be boys. In real life, as well? No doubt males have had, and still do, even at this stage of human development, a greater propensity for violence. Is it culture, genes, testosterone? A wise combination, probably, like everything that happens to human beings.

We Need to Talk about Kevin is a novel by North American writer Lionel Shriver, which was the inspiration for a bad film. The book, however, is good. And terrifying.

The novel is written in the first person. The mother writes letters to the absent father. Their surname, Katchadourian, is an excellent choice: it references an Armenian family, lending vibrancy and life to a family story. All the action is scrupulously dated and related to the country's political history; every fact takes place in a specific neighborhood, in a well-defined, well-described place. Oh, the precision of the novel! Is it possible to get around that?

Eva, Kevin's mother, isn't an average woman, an average mother. The son is a monster right from birth, but she's the only one who knows it. Or is she the cause? Eva doesn't love her son. She carries out everything that's expected of a mother with mechanical correctness, but she recognizes the profound insincerity of that imitation of a love she doesn't feel. Does Eva not love her son because from the very first she understands that Kevin is a monster, or vice-versa?

That reminds me of another novel on this subject, which is already beginning to form a thematic subgenre, that of troublesome children. (But aren't they all?). It's Doris Lessing's *The Fifth Child*. What is he, what is that fifth child who comes to subvert, to deform, the family's happiness? The sequel, *Ben in the World*, disappointed me. The doubt is resolved; the story veers toward science fiction, and Ben turns out to be a strange combination of ancient genes, a sort of hominid predating *Homo sapiens*. On the other hand, it was fascinating to think of him as just one more child, yet different, fighting, from the time of the pregnancy itself, against that mother's foreign, threatening body, a body alien to the one who feeds on it.

Let me get back to Kevin's mother, a great character. She's a woman who is hard on herself, aware of her mistakes and her shortcomings, her coldness and her lack of genuine love for her son. Her entire capacity for passion is vested in the relationship with her husband, and, later, in her love for her younger daughter. The mother in my novel, however, oscillates between confusion and despondency, doesn't understand the world around her, doesn't understand what's going on with her daughter. In general terms, she doesn't understand. She loves Natalia boundlessly, with an oppressive, constant, irrevocable love.

For the effects of the party at Pilar's house, I used facts from a real situation. On a certain occasion I had to go to a hall where my daughters' end-of-year school party had been held, because one of them had lost her wallet. I was greeted by the owner and a partner, two people my own age. Disgusted and furious, and attacking me as if I were personally responsible for the mess, they took me to see the room where the party had been. For the first time, I understood why my daughters never accepted my suggestions to have a party at home, a *potluck*, as I called it, using the vocabulary and innocence of a sixties teenager. In addition to other disasters (the chaos and destruction those kids had wreaked with a fire hose was indescribable), the floor of the hall was literally covered to an eight-inch depth with a couple of layers of bottles, flasks, beverage cartons. It was hard to imagine how and where the partygoers moved or danced. The scene wouldn't have helped me make literary choices, however: it was frightening, but above all, it was unrealistic.

White Powder

Natalia slogged through high school with an indifference that Esmé found painful and Guido found natural. Sudden sparks of interest would appear. Natalia would appear to be momentarily enthusiastic about a class, a subject, a professor, and Esmé would rekindle her illusions once again In her imagination, it was merely a question of finding a vocation. Once launched in the proper direction, like an arrow that invariably hits the bull's eye, Natalia would have a brilliant, glamorous destiny. Natalia was so bright, so extraordinary, that the world couldn't help recognizing it.

When Natalia tried out for the school's hockey team, Esmé hurriedly studied the rules of the game, which now fascinated her. How was it possible that she had never before become interested in such an exciting sport? For three months she imagined Naty traveling around the world with the Argentine national team, scoring the best goals, acclaimed in stadiums and featured on the cover of every magazine. The same thing happened with tennis, but to an even greater degree, because as a tennis champion, she wouldn't have to share her success with a team, which, when it came down to it, would only have put a burden on her talent. Then came swimming. Guido, with his chameleon-like personality, his natural penchant for blending in with his chosen surroundings, at least super-ficially (a pretty peel with no fruit, Esmé now thought), understood his daughter's fleeting passions much better than Esmé; he was less concerned about her fickleness and bought her the best Swiss racquets, ordered the most sophisticated hockey sticks from South Africa, trophies that he wouldn't allow to be resold when her passion de-clined, because where there once was fire, ashes remain, and at any moment now she could start again, Guido insisted, so they languished in piles in the storage room where Natalia and Esmé lived after the separation, along with the old painting equipment Guido had brought back from Paris, things that had survived the jumble sale in which he had gotten rid of most of his trappings: an easel, an unfinished sketch, and a handful of brushes and spatulas that he didn't want to use but didn't want to give away, either.

A strange law that pegged the value of local currency to the dollar had made foreign products quite accessible. Guido's textile business (or little workshop), oppressed by the competition of imports, had been reinvented, like so many others, firing its few workers and concentrating on importing clothing from China. As a militant busi-nessman, Guido explained to his partner (who spent his time singlehandedly contending with customers, sup-pliers, and suits over damages) how important it was to participate in meetings of the Clothing Industry Associa-tion and the Federation of Industrial Textiles. While his friend struggled to keep the business afloat, Guido, sport-ing Dolce & Gabanna or Calvin Klein jeans and Tommy Hilfiger or Ralph Lauren tee shirts, played paddle ball with other aspiring entrepreneurs. Or, at least, that's how he was seen from that most terrible of vantage points, the merciless eyes of a betrayed ex-wife.

Esmé sometimes envisioned her daughter as a scientist who would revolutionize genetics (God knows why, but it was always genetics rather than any other scientific field). On other occasions, rereading her school papers (she had kept all Naty's notebooks), she imagined her as a talented novelist, respected by critics and celebrated by the public. She saw her as the captain of a warship, or conquering Himalayan peaks that had never before been scaled (not even by the Sherpas themselves). Couldn't Esmeralda's own destiny have been different if she had been born at another time in the history of the country, of the world? Her generation had been so badly punished. Dictatorship, exile, one economic catastrophe after another ... The first democratic government, which had ended in chaos, and the anguish of hyperinflation. After a brief spring, the recession once again weighed the country down.

"Because, really," Esmé said when she and her friends discussed their children, the main topic of professional women's conversation, in spite of everything, "what do we want for our children? The simplest and most difficult thing – for them to be happy!"

And they all nodded approval and sighed, repeating: that's the only thing we want for our children, for them to be happy! They were lying, of course.

Poor children, Esmé thought, because they too had endured something like that in their own day: exhausted and sweaty, they had borne the burden of their parents' self-esteem. She realized that she saw her daughter through a mother's eyes, different from, but hardly less cruel than, the eyes through which she saw Guido, the look that she had never thought she'd acquire: so hard, so demanding, always ready to uncover the tiniest imperfection, only to try to conceal it immediately from the eyes of the world. Or just the opposite. During an advertising campaign for a burger chain, Esmé had attended several motivational group meetings in which mothers were asked to describe their children. Curiously, the first thing that emerged was a kind of competition among the mothers to prove which of them had the most rebellious, most difficult, most disobedient, neglectful, violent, or complicated sons or daughters. As if they needed to demonstrate to one another and to the world the enormous difficulties they had to face in their burdensome, arduous task of motherhood. Speaking ill of one's children is like spitting at heaven, Alcira would say. And maybe in Alcira's generation, Alcira's, the era of hypocrisy *par excellence*, when other people's opinions were serious, unchangeable, and damning, mothers restricted themselves to praising their kids. Now, however, it took the intervention of a group therapist, using specific questions, to drag something positive out of those women, a description of some praiseworthy quality in the awful children they seemed to have been saddled with and about whom they felt guilty.

Advertising, too, had changed a great deal in the last few years. Esmé, who always had an ironic bent, realized that only now was it possible to record certain commercials that she had been proposing since the seventies. Humor now had begun to dominate the screen, sometimes offbeat humor, though it still would have been impossible to produce that series she had once imagined for a denture adhesive: Sergeant Baxter and his false teeth, nailed to the fuse of a grenade. Tarzan swinging from vine to vine with the knife between his teeth, then grabbing the knife in his fist with the dentures sticking to the blade. When it came to hygiene-related products, cosmetics, baby food, cars, and diapers, such raw humor was still not admissible, but it was expanding nicely in the realm of other advertised products. In any case, Esmé was now very pleased to be a creative director, with the authority to absorb, utilize, and sell her young teams' creativity as her own. There were a few modern commercials she simply didn't understand, ideas that seemed strange and alien to her. It was hard for her to get used to the loss of certain norms that had seemed immovable and eternal, like the need to repeat the product's name as many times as possible, whereas these days it might never be mentioned at all. She worked in a smaller agency now, earning less than she had a few years before, and she knew that her days in advertising were numbered.

Cell phones were still a small luxury when Natalia was in her third year of high school, but she owned one. The nineties were coming to an end, and all the illusions and fantasies that Guido had invested in his business, plus all the work and commitment his partner had contributed, were dissipating into thin air. Nonetheless, he still had enough money left over to give his daughter that birthday gift. On condition, of course, that Esmeralda pay for the monthly service. Esmé's income had dwindled, and it wasn't just a question of age. With the country's economy at a standstill, the brilliant lights of the advertising industry were the first to go out little by little. Commercials were being filmed now, budgets had been cut, fewer print ads were published, salaries fell. Even Alcira's foreign currency savings, which had seemed eternal, had been decimated by the hyper-evaluation of the Argentine peso, and Natalia's grandmother was starting to worry.

It was through the cell phone, then, that Natalia's voice reached Esmé.

"Mamá, I have a problem. You'll have to go to school tomorrow. You and Papá. I'll explain later."

That night Natalia seemed down, preoccupied. Until then she had usually displayed a sunny disposition, in spite of the fact that now she wore the dark shades of adolescence, especially black and gray. At Esmé's high school, back in the sixties, uniforms had been required, and there were few things she and her classmates hated more than the pleated gray skirts, light blue shirts, and contrasting blue sweaters that they were obliged to wear day after day. On one of those long-ago days, the girls in her grade had all agreed to wear red sweaters, in wild, daring defiance of institutional rules. Now, when there were hardly any schools left that required uniforms, not even the white smocks once associated with State high schools, the mobs of kids thronging around the high school, when seen from a distance, looked a little like a storm cloud, which on closer view resolved into a crowd of identically dressed boys and girls, voluntarily uniformed in jeans or sweat pants, dark (always dark) hoodies, and sneakers (always sneakers), curiously sitting on the sidewalk because it was no longer a *sine qua non* to wear neatly pressed or even clean clothing, and these kids' garments required no special care whatever. Young people wore neon colors to raves, but in general, bright, warm, intense, happy colors, red, yellow, turquoise, orange, had become a sign of late adulthood, pathetically identified with garish old ladies.

Upbeat Naty, always ready to share details about her day at school, and especially entertaining when she talked about Rita, her bosom buddy and the permanent target of her funniest, most biting criticism, was replaced that evening by a girl who seemed older, self-absorbed, one who regarded the *pastel de papas* on her plate with the scrutiny of someone who detested grapes, as if she were prepared to track each one down and remove it. And that was exactly what she began to do.

"But Natalia, you've always loved them!"

"I don't anymore," said Natalia, gloomily. "They look like flies."

"Why do we have to go to the school tomorrow?"

"To talk to the principal. At eleven o'clock. It's important. I've got a headache, Mamá."

And it was impossible to extract more information from her.

Early the next morning a phone call from the secretary confirmed what Natalia had told them. But at eleven Esmeralda was expected to present an ad campaign for a new antiperspirant that was being promoted as intensely masculine, with the objective of selling it to women, a strange, modern, though not ridiculous paradox, whose practical reality had been borne out by marketing surveys. Guido tried to beg off but finally consented to take over.

Esmé' had finished her commitment at work, including lunch with the client, and was on her way home, when she received the call.

"I'm coming over," Guido said. "I want you to check Natalia's room."

"And look for what?"

"I don't know. Anything that strikes you as unusual."

"I'm supposed to ransack the room when she isn't there? I'm supposed to be responsible for the worst, most screwed-up actions, as usual? I'm the one who's supposed to confront her, set limits, and discipline her, and you're the good guy who spoils her and gives her gifts on weekends?"

"Okay, we'll do it together," Guido sighed, with good reason to be fed up and little desire to argue. "I'll be there in fifteen minutes."

They didn't have to search very long. At the back of the wardrobe, barely concealed by a shoe box, was a transparent little plastic baggie, unlabeled, containing about fifty grams of white powder.

Esmé burst into tears. Trembling, for the first time in years she allowed herself to be embraced by Guido, who was breathing hard, almost panting.

Guido told her all about the excruciating meeting with Pippi Wrongstocking, as the kids called the school principal, alluding to the only concession to fashion the woman allowed within the confines of her elegant, but classic, wardrobe: her vast array of stockings, usually some variety of fishnet, embellished with rhinestone appliqués.

Wrongstocking expressed regret that Natalia's mother hadn't come. With her was a tutor who introduced himself as Lucas. After many false starts, like someone trying to advance toward a goal while at the same time wanting to avoid it, contradictory and confused, the teacher spoke of Natalia but said nothing new, nothing that many others hadn't already said: she talked about her beauty, her friendliness, the sway she held over her classmates ... but then the speech veered toward the disturbing zone, the zone she both wanted and didn't want to reach: she spoke of kids today, of adolescence, the nineties, the lack of values, the responsibility that they, the adults, had; she asked if they had detected or observed changes in Natalia's behavior; she moved in and out, going around in circles, till Guido abruptly asked her if she was referring to drugs, if that was what she meant, what she was telling him, that his daughter was addicted to drugs, to a particular drug or to many or all of them, or in any case which ones. The principal looked at Lucas, a relatively young man, and he returned her look with concern, as though wanting to forge ahead. Guido couldn't help wondering what failures, what calamities, what addictions could have made a young man like Lucas, over thirty and with a cultured diction that suggested an advanced education, a middle-class home, accept a job as tutor – a miserable job with a miserable salary – at this stage of his life.

In short, what Guido told Esmé was that at his meeting with the principal, they hadn't accused Natalia of being a drug addict, but rather a dealer, of carrying out a system of transactions in which she didn't have a direct, personal role, but instead acted as a small capitalist with other kids in her employ. One of them had been ratted out by his classmates, and it had been proved that he was carrying on his person something he shouldn't have been carrying (neither the principal nor Lucas was very specific in this regard). In turn, the boy accused Natalia of being the mastermind of a modest trafficking network in the school, in which he was collaborating against his will, or at least against his principles, motivated and in a way exonerated, at least in his own eyes, by love.

Guido knew right away who the boy they were referring to probably was, as did Esmé when she heard the story. Natalia had often spoken to them of Lautaro, dull, good-natured, boring Lautaro, who relentlessly and hopelessly pursued her.

"He wanted revenge," Esmé said.

"That's what I told them, Guido assured her, "but they didn't want to listen to me. Lautaro is a very good student. You know how educators are: if a kid gets good grades and doesn't make trouble, they put him on a pedestal. They don't realize those are sometimes the worst ones, the ones that show up one day at gym class with a machine gun."

In effect, the meeting continued almost as if they hadn't heard a word he said, Guido added.

"It's not necessary to make a scandal that will slander your daughter," the principal had explained. "We suggest that Natalia drop out of school discreetly, with some excuse. Maybe a family trip, you decide. Otherwise she'll be dismissed for unacceptable conduct. She would have to pass all her classes in order to return to school, and we hope she won't try."

Naturally there was no way she would be expelled; they could rest easy in that regard, said Wrongstocking. No danger of an expulsion that might complicate Natalia's enrollment at another institution; no way did they want to complicate the future – doubtless a good one, a promising one – of one of their students over a mere slip, an adolescent's foolishness, a situation that certainly could be reversed with her parents' intervention. But they didn't want to keep her, either, not at present, not at the school, not among their students.

Esmé hated herself for missing that meeting, for having left Guido with the responsibility of that conversation which he surely hadn't known how to manage properly. She would have done it much, much better; she would have persuaded Wrongstocking that Natalia was being unfairly, very unfairly, accused by a boy who had nothing to lose by foisting his real, concrete guilt onto someone else. Why hadn't she been at that meeting and all the others, why hadn't she been present at so many other moments in her daughter's life, a life that now ran the risk of being lost forever, of disintegrating into millions of tiny flecks, like that damn white powder.

And without saying it, without looking at one another, but holding one another up by the hand and simultaneously accusing each other of what was happening to their poor Natalia, they remembered their own first experiences with marijuana, which they both still smoked occasionally. Esmé couldn't help thinking (as she told Guido for the first time) about the supplier of white powder who stopped by the agency with the same regularity, though with less frequency, as the vendors of those art books which had now been replaced by the Internet. Even Esmé had tried it, but only once (and she didn't tell this to Guido because she didn't want to hear his accusations, his sarcastic remarks); she had sniffed that white powder, which didn't produce any effect other than a kind of mental clarity, as if someone had suddenly turned on a light in her mind, which (but she hadn't know it till this very moment) was really in shadow.

Both of them knew, and they considered it, weighed it, that the new generations, not just adolescents, but people in general, perhaps not all of them, but certainly many people who were ten or fifteen years their juniors, used drugs for work or recreation without necessarily being addicts, but that acceptance became useless, became a lie, when it had to do with their daughter, their Natalia, with that mystery Natalia had become, endangered, Esmé thought, always at the edge of the abyss, perhaps even in that abyss by now. Guido was becoming angry, upset.

"Same as always," he yelled at Esmé. "You're psychotic, demented! Your head's always worked the same way, just like when you thought Naty was going to fall out the window and you wanted to keep us in the dark, with the blinds lowered, like the maniac you are! Nothing's wrong with Natalia. That wasn't even what they told me. There's nothing wrong with her at all!"

Then Natalia arrived.

At first it was a complete surprise: it was very strange, very unusual for her father to be in the house where she lived with her mother. But just one look at Esmé's red eyes, at Guido's out-of-control expression, was enough for her to understand.

"War council ... you talked to Wrongstocking. What did that witch tell you? Did she make something up to milk you for more money? Does she need new pantyhose?"

"I did the talking," The terrible baggie with the white powder was on top of the table. "What is this?"

"You went through my room!" Natalia shouted. And tears began to well up, not quite spilling over, clinging to the surface and making her honey-colored eyes even more beautiful. "I never, ever thought you guys would do that. That you were *those* kind of parents ... You were the ones who taught me that ..."

"What is this, Natalia?" Guido asked sharply, trying to circumvent the trembling explanations that Esmé was about to attempt.

"Try it. Try it, both of you."

"You're crazy!" Guido shouted.

Esmé was shaking; her teeth chattered.

Natalia licked a finger to moisten it, swiped it through the white powder and brought it to her mouth again. Guido and Esmé, surprised, did the same.

"It's ... sweet," said Guido.

"It's ... it's ... it's powdered sugar!" said Esmé. And she burst out crying again.

"Rita and I wanted to play a trick on that dumb Lucas ... Did you meet Lucas today, Papá? He's always poking his nose around in our business, looking for what isn't there! I should have reported him for ... for ... He has no right, does he? You're practically a lawyer, Papá. Don't I have any legal protection?"

But despite their enormous relief, Guido and Esmé couldn't breathe easily yet: it was just partial relief, addressing only what they had discovered in their daughter's room, not the meeting at Wrongstocking's office, the contents of which Guido now related to Natalia, trying not to lend an accusatory tone to his voice, waiting, hoping, for her defense, with the illusion that just as the alleged cocaine in the baggie had dissolved into the air of his imagination, so too would those (surely unfair) accusations they were using to persecute her.

Natalia was taken slightly aback. She probed a little more, bit her lower lip, and look at the ceiling, as if asking heaven for assistance to deal with the stupidity, incomprehension, and madness of the adult world.

"Lautaro, of course," she said. "It was Lautaro, that liar, that miserable worm. And you believe him over me? You believe anybody who accuses me of anything more than you believe me?"

No, of course not: her parents didn't believe anybody more than they did her; they believed her, Natalia, their daughter, most of all. They believed her words, her eyes.

Then Esmé uttered the only question that was really driving her mad:

"But you, Naty … you … look me straight in the eye and tell me the truth … you …"

"I'll tell you the truth, Mamá. You know you can trust me." Natalia looked at her with her innocent, sincere eyes, holding her gaze. "I'm not saying I've never smoked a joint. You probably did it, too. But cocaine doesn't interest me; it's not my thing. I've got nothing to do with that. Nothing. And besides, I know who sells it at school, but I won't say because I'm not a snitch. Longstocking's been swallowing bull."

"All right, Guido said," if they insist on expelling you, we'll file a legal appeal."

"I don't know, Papá. Do you think that's a good idea?" asked Natalia, taking a seat, now ready to have a reasonable conversation about a situation that had changed completely. "Do I have to stay in a place where people suspect me, where they don't want me?"

Esmé looked at both of them, upset, without offering an opinion.

"Yes, of course you have to stay!" Guido shouted in a voice that admitted no discussion. "If you leave now, it's like saying you're guilty."

"You're right, Papito," said Natalia, thinking it over for a moment. "We'll fight this together!"

But the legal complaint was unnecessary; the threat alone was sufficient. A private school doesn't want scandals, especially if they're drug-related. So that she wouldn't lose all her ground, Wrongstocking talked about her policy of trust and second chances, and while not exactly withdrawing the accusation altogether, she mentioned the possibility of an error, letting it be known, especially in a private meeting with Natalia in which her parents weren't present, that there would be no second chance, and that she was prepared (though Natalia didn't believe her) to take the complaint to the police.

The one who discreetly dropped out of school was Lautaro.

JOURNAL ENTRY 18

Without writing down a word, I mentally tried many ways of working out the scene and conversation with the principal. I didn't want to repeat the same process throughout the novel: a person who's not part of the family discusses Naty's conduct with her parents. And yet, this will keep happening because it's part of the theme of the novel. From within and from without, with eyes open and closed. Given the delicate information that the principal had to communicate, direct dialogue might have degenerated into an unbearable conversation, long and complicated, very hard to manage. I don't like to use stilted, neutral language in dialogues, but neither do I want to use trendy words and expressions. With Guido's indirect report, I found a way to avoid certain pitfalls, only certain ones (pitfalls: writing and navigating, of course). The story is always told from Esmé's point of view, but for God's sake, Guido is the girl's father and an essential piece of the puzzle that is her life.

Where and how I write this book: only in the morning and in the back room, which once belonged to my oldest daughter. After noon, for some strange reason, my mind goes fallow. I can write notes for newspapers or magazines, answer mail or do interviews. But I cannot, in any way, write fiction: it simply doesn't happen.

I don't bring anything tempting with me to the back room (which I pompously refer to in interviews as "my study"), nothing that might divert me from this slow, not altogether pleasant task, the first, laborious, draft, which I would gladly use any excuse, any distraction, to avoid. I don't have WinLinez here (nor do I want to download it from the Internet), the only computer game that interests me and to which I'm addicted. In this room I keep my poetry library, my collection of Latin American literature and popular literature (anonymous, from the oral tradition), but I never bring in the book I'm reading at the moment. During breaks – always necessary – I read only the Bible. Very slowly, and always in the morning; I advance gloriously, completely forgetting what I've left behind, because that's what reading is like after you turn sixty. It often happens, when you're writing a novel, that everything you read, everything happening around you, everything people tell writers about, whatever you imagine, see, or hear, somehow or other turns into material for the book in progress. In Ecclesiasticus (not to be confused with Ecclesiastes), 16, 1-3, today I read the following:

> Desire not a multitude of unprofitable children, neither delight in ungodly sons.
>
> Though they multiply, rejoice not in them, except the fear of the Lord be with them.
>
> Trust not thou in their life, neither respect their multitude: for one that is just is better than a thousand; and better it is to die without children, than to have them that are ungodly.

But is Natalia really a bad daughter? A daughter who has no fear of God? How can we be sure? She's still so young.

Project Happiness

There weren't many people in the world with whom Esmé could share the state of terror and confusion in which she had been left by the possibility that her daughter might be trapped in the white nets of cocaine. Only a few close, dear female friends who also had teenage children and who were as beside themselves as she was. It's not my thing, Natalia had said, and those terrible words flashed on and off in her head like a neon sign (but neon signs were practically obsolete). Had she tried it, then? Had she tried it and rejected it? It was impossible to discuss this with her mother, who was much more distant from the issue than she was, who had no idea what it was about, who didn't know or believe or couldn't comprehend that so many people, without being addicts, willingly used drugs as a way of being in the world, just as people her age, Alcira's, had used amphetamines to study all night long or to keep from falling asleep while driving, or to stave off hunger, or to get through a day's work after a sleepless night, but never – it must be admitted – never just for recreation, because that was what humanity's ancient recourse – the joy of alcohol (which in any case they drank in moderation) – was for. If Esmé had ever discussed drugs with her mother, it was in general terms, a current topic of interest, like insecurity or the conflict in the Middle East.

Alcira associated the drugs with other disturbing customs of modern adolescence.

"You can relax about your daughter," she said to Esmé. She didn't get any tattoos. And she doesn't hang rings in her nose or mouth like so many girls I see in the streets."

"That has nothing to do with anything, Mamá," Esmé tried to explain.

But she, too, was surprised and pleased by her daughter's decision to stand out from the rest of her generation. Natalia said she didn't want to be recognized by her tattoos. Esmé wondered if, in a girl her age, not being inked wasn't a way of making herself easily recognizable. But she didn't say it because she was very glad that there were no marks to defile Natalia's beautiful, soft skin.

"Drugs are a one-way street. Drugs kill," Alcira said, repeating what she saw on well-intentioned, but disappointing TV ads, which, in the zeal for prevention, didn't consider the possibility of recovery. If her friends' granddaughters had that *sickness*, the grandmothers didn't know or didn't tell.

"In this country militancy killed lots more people than drugs," Esmé snapped back. And there was no arguing with that.

Nonetheless, even though she knew many people who, in fact, used drugs of their own free will, she had also seen how that will could bend to the force of drugs. She had seen friends, acquaintances, colleagues, whose personalities had come undone, had crumbled, because of that beautiful, terrible powder that helped them generate the most brilliant ideas or endure hours of solitary labor, or whoop it up at parties, or simply keep on binge-drinking without side effects. The pleasure, though, didn't seem to last long; soon they'd become paranoid, aggressive, and digressive, their imaginations constantly branching out in different directions; they were capable of following all roads at the same time, never managing to focus their attention for more than a few seconds, and especially, unable to stop talking, obsessively returning to the subject that had taken over their feverish minds. Any excuse was enough to trigger mentioning the powder, its white color, or anything else that the words "white" or "powder" might evoke: snow, a blank sheet of paper, sheep, a feather duster, and they would laugh conspiratorially at these infinitely amusing jokes, which, to the others, those who weren't high, just seemed stupid, while those omnipotent geniuses, ten-minute rulers of the world, found them wonderful, hilarious. Was that what her daughter was like? Was her Natalia like that, her Naty, so very young, such a child? Like that friend of Guido's who still called her sometimes, her voice deformed into a sort of incurable cold due to a perforated septum? *Silver Nose*, one of the traditional names for the devil.

As far as Guido was concerned, once the idea of a legal appeal had been set aside, the matter was over, no more than a three-point tremor on the Richter Scale that had hardly affected their lives: no buildings, no certainties, had been upended. Once the little crisis had passed, they went back to their usual distance. There was nothing to talk about.

Through a friend, Esmé found out about Project Happiness, a non-residential rehab program. It was very expensive, but it would be worthwhile to check it out, her friend assured her without prying, respecting Esmé's privacy. There was no reason to involve anyone else in the matter; the first step was to attend some (free) meetings for parents that would acquaint them with the program's approach and listen to other parents with problems. But, was Esmé a mother with problems? Natalia attended school as usual, fulfilled the minimum requirements to maintain her enrollment, didn't take more subjects than normal, and had, as always, many friends. True, ever since her confession that she smoked a joint every once in a while and her parents' reaction (or, rather, their lack of reaction, as they didn't consider marijuana a dangerous drug), Natalia had started smoking on the balcony of her house (it was so much safer for her to smoke at home and not in the street, where she would be at the mercy of the police). Ever since then, it had been hard to talk to her. With half-closed eyelids and dilated pupils, she emitted inappropriate little giggles that drove Esmé out of her mind but which didn't manage to upset Guido, who considered it just another occupational hazard of adolescence. Esmé recalled her own teenage years, when drugs were so much harder to find and one had to make do with what was available (Skinny Sivi dosing himself with amphetamines, the unforeseeable effects of Benzedrine, the night when Horseface went blind for a few hours after experimenting with ethyl chloride), and she was intermittently reassured by Guido's indifference, when it didn't drive her crazy. Sometimes she thought that *she* was responsible, perhaps the only one responsible for Natalia's crossing the firepit of adolescence and reaching the other side, alive, well, and without lasting consequences.

Project Happiness occupied a house in the heights of Villa Crespo, accessible through an iron gate that opened onto a traditional, timeworn, and slightly dirty marble staircase. Parents' meetings were held in the main hall. Project Happiness was exorbitant. Perhaps that was why they offered hesitant parents three free sessions where the administration tried to persuade them that:

a) their children really *were* drug addicts; and
b) only Project Happiness could save them.

Esmé was surprised to find herself surrounded by some well-known parents, people from TV or politics. She had imagined that those highly visible parents would seek out greater discretion, private treatments. When the talk began, she realized that many of those present, both the unknown and the famous, had already gone through the experience of private treatment, some had also gone through the experience of hospitalization, and now they were here, once more hungry for hope, ready to be convinced that a new opportunity was about to open up for them, for their children.

As in Alcoholics Anonymous groups, the two women who conducted the group, a psychologist and a physician, had suffered similar situations with their own children; they were intelligent, sensitive people, and they made no promises. They merely offered reality: a twenty percent rate of cure, or recovery, or recuperation, or whatever you wanted to call it.

"If any of you ever smoked marijuana as adolescents, forget it. That experience has nothing to do with what your kids are doing," one of them said. Today's marijuana has three times more active ingredient, THC, tetrahydrocannabinol, than in your day."

But Esmé hadn't just smoked marijuana as a teenager, when *maconia* (it came from Brazil, and that was what they called it) was still pretty rare and hard to find. Like many parents of her generation, although she hadn't smoked much, she had only given up marijuana altogether relatively recently, after a bad reaction that spiked her pulse to 140 for several hours and precipitated a panic attack. It was true that the experience was completely different, especially because then she was a daughter and now she was a mother. Esmé doubted and doubted, envying the conviction of other people with less familiarity and more clarity, more drive, more decisiveness, people like her mother, who was able to divide the world into black and white. When she began listening to the other parents relate their experiences, the tangle, instead of organizing itself into a careful row of certainties, became even knottier.

A young mother, separated, who looked younger than forty, told a terrifying story: how she confirmed her suspicions that her twelve-year-old son was a cocaine addict the day she asked him to help clear the table and the boy replied with a punch that left her with a bloody nose. Her son attended a private school, a combination of primary and secondary, where an older classmate sold him the drug.

The group coordinators explained that Project Happiness wasn't easy and that it demanded a very high level of commitment on the parents' part. It wasn't just a question of daily visits to the hospital, to which they had to bring their children, even against their will, dragging them in by force or threatening to call the police if necessary. It was also essential, obligatory, to separate the addict from all relationships that had led him to this situation. They had to pull him out of school, take away all his money, forbid contact with old friends, rip posters of musical groups that reminded him of the most pleasant aspects of addiction from his walls. They had to keep him under control, and, if necessary, locked up, night and day, banning all unauthorized outings. One mother explained how she had locked her son in his room with a key and how that same night he escaped through the window. The next step was to board up the windows.

A husband and wife (the man wore bangs and sixties-style glasses that had gone out of style many years before) related how they thought they had managed to protect their son from all harm. The boy didn't go out for more than half an hour per day, to walk the dog. Until one day they realized that the dog-walkers' trail was precisely where the transactions were made. There was a meeting point in a square close to their house, and the boy bought the substance that, despite his apparent docility, he continued to consume.

Of all the Project Happiness stratagems that Esmé considered impossible to fulfill, one of the most difficult was the requirement to remove posters of her daughter's favorite bands from the walls. She envisioned herself walking into Natalia's room and yanking, tearing like a madwoman at those posters from which unfamiliar men and women stared at her. (Esmé was incapable of distinguishing or recognizing the bands her daughter listened to, which she sometimes mistakenly called "musical groups"), while Natalia stared at her, wide-eyed and disconcerted.

At the second meeting, the coordinators introduced a mother and daughter whom they considered to be one of the Project's great successes. Greatly surprised, Esmé recognized one of Natalia's kindergarten classmates. The mother described how one afternoon she had gone to pick up her daughter, who was coming out of a club. She arrived slightly before the appointed pick-up time and found her with a group of friends, smoking marijuana. Without a moment's hesitation, she grabbed the joint from her hand, shoved her into the car, and the next day, with the girl locked in her room, she sought out and found information about Project Happiness. The daughter gazed at her mother with appreciation, with love, and as they told of their experience, both of them continually smoked tobacco cigarettes, kindling the desire to smoke in other parents, who in turn added their own smoky contribution, until the whitish fog grew thick and the air, unbreathable.

A desperate father tearfully confessed that he was participating in the program alone, in the hope that they could help him. His daughter was living on the streets. Up to her neck in the madness of addiction, not to just one drug, but to several simultaneously (which was really more common, as Esmé was discovering), she had been recruited into prostitution by an organization that dealt in human trafficking.

A young woman with dyed-blonde hair, who must have been around thirty-five, tapped her foot rhythmically on the floor in a state of psychomotor excitement. Only when she started to speak did Esmé notice the elderly couple, modestly dressed and in old-fashioned clothes, sitting beside her. In an environment where anguish and guilt were the most widely shared feelings, the hatred in the girl's voice stood out. She was there to try to help her husband, and she complained bitterly about her in-laws' lack of understanding, as they were the only ones who had his chance for salvation in their hands, and yet they had abandoned him to his drug use. The two old folks began to speak. They presented their case, interrupting one another, heartbroken, and in a thick Galician accent.

"He has that sickness, but he's our son. What can we do?" they said. "We love him just the same!"

"But it's bad kind of love! You don't control his money. He shouldn't be able to get his hands on money! Don't you realize what he's using it for?"

"And how, for God's sake, are we going to control his money?" the old folks wondered. "He's the one in charge of the business!"

They looked fragile, they didn't understand, and they tried to fend off the waterfall of fury that their daughter-in-law unleashed on them. She was trying to save her partner, but if she failed, she would walk away, Esmé thought. The parents, on the other hand, would remain chained to their son, sick or well, unto death.

After the three meetings spent listening to stories so different from her own, Esmé was convinced that Natalia had told the truth. She occasionally smoked marijuana, but cocaine, "wasn't her thing," whatever that meant. And Project Happiness demanded more than what Esmé could or would carry out under those circumstances.

JOURNAL ENTRY 19

Is it valid to narrate a novel in episodes? But even if it's organized (or disorganized) into episodes, a novel could have a plot. Life, however, has no plot. And so I appeal to one of the oldest, most frequent and shopworn resources, the same justification that has been used to explain the need for naturalism, surrealism, the theater of the absurd: the rediscovery of reality.

Literature is always artifice, words that can only *seem*, but never *be* true, because the truth, that curious construct, is not found in discourse, but in facts, in the mysterious, elusive, perhaps nonexistent past. That's why every literary tendency has always claimed to be much more realistic than the cult of what's known as realism.

The novel, poor thing, doesn't offer many options in this regard: it contains either a plot or a voyage. Ever since *The Odyssey*, the voyage is the greatest stratagem for linking episodes. In the picaresque novel, the main character goes from one master to another, as in my own novel, *Laurita's Loves,* in which the protagonist moves from one man to another. A life story is a voyage through time. If I want it to be more than a rosary of episodes strung together by a thread, I have to make sure my characters grow and change.

In order to get information about Project Happiness, I spoke to my cousin B., who once attended one of those parental meetings and luckily didn't have to go beyond that. The other parents' stories convinced her that her son's situation wasn't that serious.

I had a few regrets about inviting her out for coffee. My cousin, a very demanding, slightly gourmand-ish sort of person, sent back the first coffee because it was cold, the second because it was burned, and drank the third very grudgingly as she told me her story.

From her experience with Project Happiness, she came to the conclusion (perhaps mistaken or not applicable in all cases) that forcing a person to participate in an out-patient hospital program was an excellent and necessary measure in cases of severe addiction, but could be negative and even cause an adverse reaction in occasional or "light" drug users. Many years had passed, her son was fine, and she wasn't sorry about her decision. She always wondered what had become of that young girl and her mother who were so proudly and desperately smoking tobacco laced with nicotine, that legal, addictive, destructive drug. Today, B. said, as she took comfort in the anti-smoking laws in cafés while holding an stubbed-out cigarette between her fingers, they wouldn't have been allowed to smoke like that, in an enclosed room.

LUNCH WITH A FRIEND

Marcos had been clear: I want to talk to you; it's important. His tone left no room for fantasies, and yet the lunch invitation gave Esmeralda that inevitable tingling sensation. Guido's former classmate was also the family physician, the one they went to when they didn't have absolute confidence in a diagnosis or their insurance company's service. On the other hand, Marcos was a married man, and Esmé had been dating a client from her agency. They weren't a formal couple yet, but she could see some potential. There was no reason for that tingling. Nevertheless, Esmé had learned from experience that when a young woman is divorced, the first to try something are the husbands of her female friends and then her husband's friends. There was a reason for that tingling.

Esmeralda knew quite well that Lucrecia, Marcos' wife, was very jealous, not of other women, but of the unhealthy job to which her husband devoted his time and his soul. Marcos had no fixed schedule and no days off, and the situation had grown worse over the past few years, because of the advent of cell phones, which many people found annoying but no one considered a fad anymore. In any case, if it was a case of discussing something important, why meet for lunch instead of inviting her to his office? Of course there was a reason for that tingling.

Choosing the right clothes for in-between seasons was always a problem. She rejected the gray dress with leather buttons: the neckline was too low, and she didn't want to feel ridiculous in a conversation that might have to do with health issues. Could Guido be ill? she pondered. Gravely ill? Did the idea pain her, make her sad, torture her? Did the idea please her? Was it something about her mother's health? she wondered, with a sudden physical reaction, a fist punching her in the stomach. But to discuss health matters, Marcos would have made an appointment with her at his office. Would Lucrecia come with him? What had always been obvious at dinner became fuzzy at lunchtime. *I* want to talk to you, not *we* want to talk to you, he had said.

When her father died, Esmé inherited a small sum that she couldn't make up her mind to invest. Marcos, one of the few high-earning physicians in Argentina, was involved in some real estate investments, possibly as a buffer against the current economic stagnation. Could that be the subject of this meeting? With Marcos and Lucrecia, then. The meeting was at a restaurant in Puerto Madero, the city's newest neighborhood, which was flourishing while the rest of the country withered. The docks on the eastern side of the dikes had been rejuvenated with brick façades; down below new restaurants were constructed, with offices above. And farther along, on the other side of the dikes, new streets, boulevards, avenues, squares, monuments, parks, and fountains were beginning to appear. An upscale neighborhood was developing to accommodate a new social class that was growing at a slower pace, though proportionately to the increase in unemployment and poverty.

Esmé decided on the red velvet suit, which was fairly formal and might even be considered daring when worn without a shirt underneath. With her Mexican silver pendant and French perfume, she felt prepared to talk about real estate deals or anything else. Maybe a little too dressed up for midday.

Esmé felt prepared for anything, but not for a face-to-face encounter with her ex as she entered the restaurant. What a damn coincidence, she thought, irritated. She greeted him with a forced smile.

"What are you doing here? Business lunch?"

"I'm meeting Marcos. And you?"

Then he'd invited both of them? How absurd. Was their mutual friend entertaining fantasies of acting as go-betweens, of setting up a meeting where they might reflect on the past, become reacquainted, get back together? Impossible. Marcos was too intelligent for that. There was just one thing that Guido and Esmeralda still had in common. Natalia. Esmé's mind started spinning wildly around her daughter's latest silences, her most recent reticence, her absences, her mysteries. Naty had been altogether hers, and now she belonged to reality, to her friends, to history, to her generation. She knew so little about her. When she shed the skin of her childhood, she also left her mother behind, her mother's body. She barely tolerated her hugs, wiped off her kisses. Esmé had lost the absolute magic of drawing out a smile; no longer was she her daughter's sun and moon; she was nothing more than an obstacle trying to insinuate its way between Naty and the world. Could Natalia have consulted Marcos without telling her? Could she be sick? Could she be pregnant? It was almost intolerable to know everything Natalia might be now. Esmé left her purse on a chair, practically gasping with anxiety, feeling her muscles and her guts go slack. No. He would have met them at his office. At his office.

As soon as she returned from the bathroom, she noticed Guido's slovenly clothing, his poorly-shaved cheeks. Or was he merely following those new norms of male elegance that her parents would have called "prisoner's whiskers?" Times had grown tough, very tough, for the businesspeople who had entered the decade of the nineties and its great opportunities so joyfully. Even importers were feeling the effects of the recession.

"Do you have any idea?" she asked him. They had been married long enough to understand one another with few words.

"Nope," Guido said. "If it was a health issue, he would have seen us at his office."

Esmé once again clung to those magic words, which she repeated silently like a mantra. At his office, at his office, at his office.

Marcos arrived with a smile, shook hands with a smile, sat down with a smile. His smile was plastic. Despite his impeccable shave, he looked much worse than Guido. He was pale and had bags under his eyes, which were red from what appeared to be a chronic lack of sleep.

"Shall we order something? An appetizer to share?" he asked.

"We're not ordering anything, Guido said. "First explain what we're doing here."

"There's no hurry; we can eat first."

"Of course there's a hurry, Marcos," Esmé cut him off. "You're our family doctor. We're frightened."

They were interrupted by a young, good-looking waiter who wore his hair tied back in a little pony tail. It wasn't so long ago that waiters were all old men, efficient and Spanish, Esmé thought. The boy carried a blackboard with a list of the dishes that weren't on the menu, and he began describing them. Guido stopped him rudely in the middle of the eggplant dressed in extra virgin, cold-pressed, San Juan olive oil.

"We want to see the executive menu."

Very pleasantly the waited pointed out the daily lunch special, ridiculously expensive in any case, on the menu. They ordered bottled still water and sparkling water, and as soon as they managed to get rid of the waiter, Guido returned to the assault, with no need for words, just his eyes nailed on his friend.

"I need help," Marcos said. "You guys are my friends. Both of you. I have no one else to turn to."

The fact that it was Marcos who needed help assuaged their nerves immediately. Esmé felt a twinge of pride struggling to emerge. One of Guido's schoolmates considered her as good a friend as he, and that meant gaining ground in the enemy camp. Marcos was the spoils of war.

"Okay, spit it out," said Guido, irritated.

The expression "to turn to" instantly suggested money.

"I don't know where to start." Marcos looked at them as if he was puzzled, as if he hadn't been the one to summon them there.

"Start at the beginning," Guido encouraged him.

"You need help? Okay, here were are, you friends, waiting to see what can be done. What kind of mess did you get yourself into? Does it have to do with that business of buying and selling apartments?"

"The beginning. That's the hardest part. I don't know if I can. It's Natalia. Three months ago she came to see me at my office."

"Is she sick?" With a hand that seemed to have a will of its own, Esmé had crumpled her napkin into a ball and was squeezing it desperately as she spoke in an even voice.

"No, no, no! She's ... she's pregnant."

Esmé's hand relaxed. In the relieved look she exchanged with Guido were sparks of their former love. Somehow, at random moments, they still loved one another through their daughter. A pregnancy, and so young. Still such a child. It was serious, but it wasn't the end of the world. An abortion would certainly be the next step. She herself had gone through something similar as an adolescent, and her parents had helped her. Poor Naty, poor little thing! Luckily she had a mother who understood.

In general Marcos' tone was that of an indisputable authority. He spoke in a firm, clear way, and he was very didactic when giving an explanation, as if he were always talking to a patient, an assembly of colleagues, or a university class. Now his words were clumsily garbled, tumbling over one another; his speech was pure confusion.

"She ... you guys are sensible people. She can't have that baby! She's crazy!"

"She's crazy?" Guido repeated. "What's wrong with you, Marcos? I'm grateful that you've told us, but this is something we have to work out as a family."

Esmé couldn't help picking up on the word *family*, not sure if she was annoyed or pleased.

"Poor baby, she must need help. She still hasn't worked up the nerve to talk to us," Esmé said.

"Well, I agree with Marcos. She's not old enough to … Do you know who the father is? Did she tell you?" Guido asked.

"That's … that's what I wanted to talk to you about. What happened was … She … Natalia is asking me for money …"

The waiter brought the beverages and the appetizer. Guido and Esmé, sitting stiffly in their chairs, were beginning to understand, though they preferred not to. Nobody had the strength to pick up a fork.

"No," said Esmé. "No. It can't be."

But it could. That explained, for example, why he had asked them to meet him in a public place and not at his office. To force them to remain under control.

"It wasn't me. I don't know how to explain it to you. I swear that … It was a … I couldn't … I couldn't resist."

He looked at Guido, begging him for understanding, complicity, but Natalia's father shot back an icy, still incredulous, stare.

"She … Don't think I was the first."

"You're blaming her? You're an adult man, a father, a doctor, and you're trying to blame a fifteen-year-old girl?"

"She's already sixteen."

"She just turned sixteen last week!"

"It's statutory rape!"

"It's not statutory rape. Under Argentine law, statutory rape is with children under thirteen."

"You looked it up, you son-of-a-bitch!"

"I had no choice, Guido, Esmeralda. I need help!"

"I'll kill you. I'll kill you."

"She's asking me for money!"

"I can imagine. Poor baby. To pay for the abortion," Esmé said. "Now I understand why it was so hard for you to confide in me this time."

"You don't understand anything. She's asking me for a lot of money not to have the baby. So she won't tell Lucrecia. She's blackmailing me!"

"You deserve it. Whatever she's asking for isn't enough."

"Please, please, help me! I already gave her ten thousand dollars! And now she's asking for fifty thousand!"

The sum mentioned shook Guido and Esmeralda a little. Even at that moment, when the dollar was still pegged to the Argentine peso, the numbers were astonishing. Lunch was over. Not one of the three of them had felt like eating. There were no arguments when Marcos called for and paid the bill.

All three of them left together. They had barely stepped on the sidewalk when Guido, who was slightly ahead, suddenly spun around and punched his former friend in the face, brutally, with a closed fist. Marcos didn't defend himself. He tottered a little and fell down on his butt, rubbing his chin and looking at them almost gratefully.

"This is you, it's all your fault," Guido said to Esmé in the taxi carrying them downtown. "You, who makes fun of everything. You've taught her not to take anything seriously. To have no values!"

"Look who's talking," Esmé retorted.

"Don't start."

"I'm not starting because it's not necessary. You already think you know everything. What I want to say to you is something else. If you blame me, it's because you're accusing her! You defended her to Marcos, and now you're the one saying that a fifteen-year-old girl is the guilty party, not the victim!"

"We have to talk to Natalia. But I need to cool off a little. To think. You're a woman – you talk to her."

Esmé prepared herself for a tough, difficult, disturbing conversation. One woman to another. She would tell Naty about her own experience, especially how she felt when her mother went with her to the abortion clinic, back in the sixties, how she held her hand while they applied the gas mask, how she felt a current of love but also of hatred circulating between those hands united by strength. Her daughter would tell her everything, or at least whatever she was able to tell her; she wouldn't try to worm anything out of her. They would speak from the heart, both of them would cry, and they'd end up with their arms around one another.

Natalia was with her friend Rita; it wasn't a good time to talk to her. Her pupils were dilated, her eyelids at half-mast, and she wore that silly, mysterious little smile that she got from marijuana. But Esmé couldn't wait. She asked her to send Rita home. Her face and gestures were anxious enough to make Natalia accept without protest.

"*Hijita*, are you pregnant?"

"No way", said Natalia, surprised.

"You know you can talk to me."

"Of course, Mamita. But, sorry, you're not having grandkids for a while yet. Where did you get the idea …? Oh, now I know! Did Marcos call you?"

"We met with him to talk. Papá was there, too."

Natalia burst out laughing. She roared with laughter.

"How messed up that shit must be, asking you for help!"

"But … then … you're not? Then why did …?"

The girl bit her lower lip and rolled her eyes, the typical gesture of her generation, which exaggerates the patience needed to deal with the naïveté of parents.

"Mamá, there's nothing easier than fooling a man. They think they rule the world! I showed him the result of a test, but it wasn't mine!"

Everything Esmé had prepared to say to Natalia vanished into thin air. She was puzzled.

"Then where did you get it from?"

"I bought it. You can get them."

"Is it true he gave you ten thousand dollars? And that you asked him for fifty thousand more?"

"But he deserved it, Mamá. Don't you think he deserved it?"

Yes, Esmé thought that Marcos deserved it. And yet.

"I'm not going to tell you what you have to do, Naty. If you think you need to talk with Marcos' wife, even if you want Papá and me to talk to her …"

And for a moment Esmé accepted her evil feelings, that another woman should suffer what she had gone through.

"But I think … I don't know, I think you should stop

asking him for money. For your own sake. For your dignity. And because it could be dangerous…"

"You know what? That's what I thought, too. I won't ask him for more, promise. But Mami, do you think I could keep the ten thousand?"

It touched Esmé that her daughter would ask, that she was asking her for permission. And it seemed to her that she should *not* keep the money. It was the least that son-of-a-bitch should have to pay, but it also was too much money for a girl her age to handle. Natalia had to understand the seriousness of what she had done.

"You'll have to return that money, Naty," she answered sternly.

Natalia made a sulking face.

"But I don't want to see Marcos again, Ma."

"Of course not. You'll give the money to your dad."

"What if he keeps it?"

"What do you mean, if he keeps it, Naty? What are you saying?"

"I'd rather give it to you."

What did Natalia know about her father that Esmé didn't? Was Guido capable of doing something like that? She had planned to have a long chat with her daughter, and now she couldn't think of anything to say.

Sometime later they learned that Marcos and Lucrecia had separated. She kept the kids and wouldn't let him see them. Marcos was filing a lawsuit to try to repair his relationship with his children.

JOURNAL ENTRY 20

When I came up with the idea for this little anecdote, the relationship between Natalia and one of her parents' friends, I knew I had hit on something interesting. A conversation with L. convinced me that I should present it as a dramatic scene. I didn't let anyone read the first, rough drafts of this book, because at that stage of writing, I'm not interested in readers' opinions. I'm aware of many obvious defects, and I know – or think I know – how to correct them, but I need to keep going so that I'll have all the raw material before starting my rewrite. Otherwise I might be reworking the first page indefinitely without ever getting into the novel. However, and as a single exception, I gave L. a first draft of this chapter. Her always-valued opinion was that the situation was too rushed, but I already knew that, and it convinced me not to show the drafts to anyone else.

Going back to my discomfort with the "string of episodes" effect, I need to be careful not to let my novel lose the only definitive quality of good literature: the ability to surprise (with its language, its selection of materials, its organization, but also in the development of the story). Am I in danger? At this point the reader can already partially foresee what's going to happen and prepares to discover what new calamity Natalia is about to provoke. I suddenly remember a book from my childhood, *The Misfortunes of Sophie*, by the Countess of Ségur, a moralistic tale for girls. Published in 1859, it was still read in Argentina one hundred years later. The countess was a Russian diplomat's daughter who went into exile in France with her family and wrote in French these little stories in which Sophie, a little girl of four or five, commits small acts of mischief that her mother forbids and punishes in a cruel, sometimes sadistic, way. My interest in Sophie's naughtiness was more than a little bit prurient; I think what kept me reading was the need to find out how her mother would punish her this time. I must admit that the episodic effect didn't diminish the readers' interest one bit.

The Unfortunate Accident

"It's important for Natalia to keep telling the truth," said Dr. Martegut.

His office, its style, the elegant neighborhood, the classy building, the blend of Chesterfield chairs and mahogany, were part of a strategy designed to intimidate certain clients and give others the feeling they'd entered an environment rich in tradition, reserve, wealth, and lineage, where they could count on the protection afforded by that powerful combination of factors. Dr. Martegut was a highly respected attorney who had agreed to take on Natalia's case almost as a favor for her father. His pale eyes and Roman-soldier-like head contributed to the total effect. He seemed like a man whose statements could not be challenged. In fact, he himself wouldn't be the one to handle the case, but rather Dr. Mertens, much younger and impeccably blonde, with her dark pantsuits and white shirts. Dr. Martegut made an occasional appearance, generally when it was time to discuss money.

It would never have occurred to Esmé to seek out a lawyer that night. When the phone rang, she awoke with her heart pounding: the dawn phone call, that horror film classic. She felt the rush of adrenaline in her veins spread through all the nooks and crannies of of her brain as if she were being injected. In a moment she was intensely awake and alert. She tried to breathe deeply and concentrate on what she was being told. In spite of her sensation of mental clarity, it was very hard for her to comprehend. A police officer, who noted her state of confusion and who probably was used to that sort of dialogue in the wee hours, repeated over and over again that her daughter was fine, that nothing had happened to her.

The first thing that crossed her mind was that there had been a virtual kidnapping. It happened fairly often. The perpetrators were generally prisoners. The less sophisticated ones found their victims in the phonebook. One night they had called her, saying that they had abducted her mother. The guy knew her first and last names and the relationship between them, and he had lots of other details, but the M.O. was so typical and had been published in the papers so many times (there were even mass mailings alerting the unwary) that Esmé didn't believe him, especially when her refused to let her speak to Alcira. Esmé hung up and immediately phoned her mother, who had gone to play Burako with some friends. The maid, terribly upset, nervously related her conversation with the alleged kidnappers. It was obvious that they'd gotten all their information from her, but Esmé still wanted to hear her mother's voice. She didn't know exactly where she was; Alcira didn't answer her cell phone (which happened with a certain frequency because she was hard of hearing); and Esmé couldn't fall asleep till Alcira called her after midnight to tell her that she was back home, brushing aside her fears. "Don't think you're gonna get rid of your mama so easily!" At the police station they explained to her that the incident didn't merit filing an official report, as the perpetrators were in prison in any case. "The boys get bored," remarked an officer on duty.

But on the Terrible Night (as Esmé had already labeled it mentally) she had no doubts. Maybe because the policeman's insistence on soothing her stirred up her anxiety: that repeated litany, "just stay calm" – which postponed the explanation of the call – was like a seismic shift moments before the lava spews. But especially because immediately afterward, he handed the phone to Naty and she could hear her voice, her dear little voice, so fiercely loved, trembling, saying, I've got a problem, Mamita. It had been so long since she called her Mamita.

"The most important thing," Dr. Mertens insisted, "is that throughout the process your daughter must stick to the same story she gave when she broke down while making her statement. It'll be our job to prove it."

With her parents' authorization, Natalia had gotten her driver's license at age seventeen. She was a very good driver. Esmé gave her the wheel with complete peace of mind, with complete joy. And not just in the crazy, overcrowded, hellish city traffic. They had driven to the coast a couple of times, and Natalia had performed like a star along the way.

On the Terrible Night, her daughter had taken the car, a lightly-used blue Volkswagen Golf that Esmé had bought at a very good price, and which was now embedded in the concrete guardrail of the Costanera Highway, partially destroyed in the crash, surrounded by bits of rubble that looked like they'd been taken from a demolition site. The VW was embedded in an almost comical way, like in a cartoon. Five blocks behind, a body lay on the ground, a covered-up body that Esmé never saw, but one which nonetheless would reappear over and over in her nightmares, sometimes with her father's face.

The car (it was the car, the car, she forced herself to think, not her daughter, not her friend Rita – it was the damn car) had leaped the sidewalk, run over that man (who, now a dead body, rested on the asphalt awaiting Forensics), continued on its way, faster and faster, beyond all speed limits, and ended up crashing against the concrete barricade.

It had been a gorgeous, perfect night. Three AM on a warm September morning. A gentle breeze, redolent of springtime, caressed her face with its cool fingers. Beyond the barricade, the dark river danced about and laughed, spilling out in playful little waves against the shore.

She had never seen her daughter look so beautiful. Natalia was shivering and her teeth chattered, but she was in one piece, hugging Rita, who was overcome by sobs. Natalia's heavily made-up eyes shone in the darkness. Her overdone makeup emphasized the childlike expression on her face.

There were many police officers, and the passing cars slowed down, trying to see what had happened. They took the girls to the station in a police car. Esmé took a taxi.

Guido went directly to the police station, accompanied by a lawyer, a very young man who, Esmé later discovered, acted as a sort of wild card, always ready to cover emergencies at Dr. Martegut's practice. It was he who assisted Natalia and accompanied her to make her statement to the D.A. Claudia, Rita's mother, embraced Esmé so tightly that she momentarily cut off her breathing; it would be the last embrace they would exchange for a long time, perhaps for the rest of their lives. Rita's father didn't show up that night.

After the statement had been given at the D.A.'s office, the young lawyer spoke with Guido and Esmé. The situation was confusing, possibly complicated. Since it was her mother's car, the court's initial assumption would be that Natalia had been driving. Even though both her father and the lawyer had advised her not to make a statement (as a defendant she was under no obligation to do so), Natalia couldn't contain herself. The girl seemed to be in shock, but instead of paralyzing her, the shock had left her in a state of heightened psychomotor excitement, very common under the circumstances. She began her statement by taking the blame for everything, almost vehemently, trying to free her friend of all guilt or involvement. "I was driving; Rita was asleep," she insisted. She seemed anxious to assume all responsibility for the deed. And yet, when the D.A. inquired about certain details provided by the police, she started making grammatical mistakes, switching from the first to third person. "Then I was going along the Costanera and she hit the gas," she said, suddenly. And at another point: "When she put it in reverse, I felt like it was running over him." (She? I? the car? It wasn't at all clear.

The D.A. was an intelligent man who had the right to suspect something more. He questioned her minutely, rigorously, and finally the girl broke down, the young lawyer told them: she burst into tears and confessed the truth. That it was Rita who was driving the Golf. That, like so many times before, she had allowed her friend to get behind the wheel of her parents' car, but please don't let her mother find out. That Rita was a great driver, even though she didn't have a license. That she, Natalia, had found it very hard to take control of the situation, that she was scared, very scared, when Rita started that crazy joyride along the Costanera.

The owner of a *choripán* and *bondiola* kiosk had seen the accident and the pedestrian trying to cross with the green light at the zebra crossing; he had seen the Golf, which seemed to come flying by out of nowhere; he had seen the impact; he had seen how the car went backward for no reason, passing over the body again and continuing on its crazed, savage way till it hit the barricade. But he didn't know for sure which of the two was behind the wheel. They were two young girls, with long, silky, dark hair, difficult to tell apart from a distance. When the police arrived, both of them had gotten out of the car and were standing together beside the car.

Later they found out that Rita's statement to the D.A had been much more confused than Natalia's. She insisted that she was in the passenger seat, that she was asleep, that she wasn't very clear on how they had run over the man, and that she didn't fully awaken till they slammed into the Costanera barricade.

Natalia wasn't present at that first meeting with Drs. Martegut and Mertens. They spoke of responsibility and of money, of the very likely civil suit, of liability insurance, of hit-and-run charges, which weren't applicable in this case, despite the insistence of the media, which had found a juicy subject to sink their teeth into.

"As you well know, Guido, since you're practically a colleague, what happened to your daughter, and I'm referring to her attempt to escape from the scene ..."

"My daughter's friend," Guido reminded him.

"Your daughter's friend … It's very common and can be explained by the state of shock caused by an accident like that. It's considered hit-and-run only if the driver runs away, leaving the victim someplace where nobody can help him."

"There are situations," Dr. Mertens recalled, "where a driver and his passenger get out of the car in the road and drag the victim to the shoulder or throw him in a ditch. That's not what happened here."

"Shall I turn on the air conditioner?" Dr. Martegut asked. "It's getting warm early this year."

He dried his perspiration, dabbing delicately at his skin with a pristine white handkerchief, the last of the white handkerchiefs, thought Esmé, who was fanning herself fiercely.

While Dr. Mertens focused on the case, Dr. Martegut let his mind wander among the multiple experiences that had marked his professional life: he had so many situations, so many anecdotes to tell, that at times he seemed to be immersed in an old man's monologue.

Those apparent, nearly intolerable amblings, which Natalia's parents could barely endure, were part of an automatic, perhaps not even deliberate *mise-en-scène* that the two attorneys carried out with exquisite coordination. Playing the old good-cop/bad-cop duo, Dr. Martegut maintained how unimportant the case was, how simple it would be to prove Natalia's innocence, the light penalty that could be predicted even for the driver of the vehicle, one to four years; they wouldn't lock her up in a juvenile detention facility, much less throw her in jail when she turned eighteen; it would certainly be a suspended sentence, intentionality made all the difference, and it was a question of involuntary, not voluntary, manslaughter. And even though Esmé trembled at the word *manslaughter*, which wasn't softened by the word *involuntary*, even though the idea of involuntary manslaughter crashed painfully against the walls of her skull, the main thing was that her daughter hadn't committed any of it, her daughter wasn't even an interested party, her daughter was as innocent as the limpid gaze of her honey-colored eyes.

Interrupting him at certain points and finishing his remarks at others, Dr. Mertens contributed the other perspective, the other possible view of the case. Dr. Martegut concentrated on how wise they had been to engage them, how easy it would be for them, thanks to his power, his knowledge, his personal friendship with the judge, to free Naty of all guilt and charges, to receive… absolution? Dismissal? Esmé added vocabulary and looked at Guido, trying to deduce from his expression what was best, in which direction to steer the bow of that foundering ship which had once been a family. And while Dr. Martegut kept commenting on the facts almost dismissively, like someone who underestimates the importance of the crumbs on the tablecloth, sweeping them away with his hand, Dr. Mertens concentrated on justifying the amount of their fees, reminding them that the first assumption would be that the vehicle owner's daughter was the one driving, that they still hadn't received the toxicology report, that the fact that the girls might have been drunk or high could be a mitigating factor, but also an aggravating one, a double edged sword in any case, depending on how the

D.A. worked the case; it could get complicated, for example, if it was proved that they routinely drove under the influence. She reminded them that the car had jumped the curb, that they had probably run over the victim's body a second time, for still-inexplicable reasons (there were witnesses, but the forensic reports weren't back yet), that they had run away, that at age seventeen they were responsible in the eyes of the law, although their situation was better than it would have been at eighteen, because they were still protected by the Convention on the Rights of the Child, that not only the marks on the pavement, but, especially, the crash against the Costanera barricade, Dr. Mertens said, allowed the experts from the Gendarmerie, in their investigation of the crash, to use scopometry (and here Dr. Martegut interrupted with an ecstatic, convoluted description of the fascinating new devices the institution now possessed) to establish the car's rate of speed, its precise speed, indicated by the degree of deformation of the metal, and that there was a possibility, remote but not out of the question, by no means out of the question, that it might be considered gross negligence, taking into account the sum total of factors: the high rate of speed, jumping the sidewalk, running over the victim twice, the fact that they were driving drunk and possibly not for the first time …

If the D.A. insisted on gross negligence and managed to prove it, the penalty could be much harsher, including the possibility of serving time. There had been cases in which a minor committed a crime prior to age eighteen, but the sentence, delivered after his birthday, treated him as a legal adult … Dr. Mertens reminded them that the sentencing judge could turn out to be especially severe; there were such types. And the media coverage of the case, even though the judge might try to avoid it, couldn't help influencing his decisions. He might decide to make an example of them, so as to keep other young people in line. In spite of everything, it might be difficult, even very difficult, to prove that it had really been Rita, and not Natalia, behind the wheel at the time of the incident, all of which explained, justified, made sense of the exorbitant fees that Dr. Martegut was quoting them now, putting an end to the conversation.

The dead man. Irreparably dead. Esmé remembered him as if she had seen him. She already knew his name and age. He was fifty-two. Two sons. He had gone to the Costanera to fish, and he was on his way home. The fishing rod and tackle box had gone flying on impact and ended up along the highway.

When they left the lawyers' office, Natalia's parents stopped for coffee to discuss what had happened, to try to come to an agreement on some essential points, to hate one another as usual and support one another, as occasionally happened. But before they could start talking about Natalia, Dr. Martegut, Dr. Mertens, and especially, about how and what they could do to come close to paying the fees, Guido looked at Esmé guiltily, sadly, a little abashedly, and told her he was leaving the country.

"Now? You're leaving now?"

"In a few days. Next month."

"But you can't!"

"What I can't do is stay here. The country is falling to pieces. We're older now. It's my last chance."

Esmé's eyes filled with tears, but her rage was greater than her fear or anxiety.

"Your last chance to act like a son-of-a-bitch? Don't believe it – you'll still have plenty of opportunities. All the days of your life."

Guido took her by the shoulders and shook her, forcing her to look at him.

"But don't you see what's happening?"

"Take your hands off me or I'll scream. You're leaving *now*? When your daughter …"

"My daughter didn't do anything. It was that friend of hers who I never liked. Naty has been unfairly accused and it'll all work out. I'm leaving you both in good hands. That gives me a little relief."

"And where are we supposed to get the money to pay those good hands? You think I'm doing so great?"

"I don't know, I don't ask you those things."

"They slashed my salary by 40%. They stopped passing out pieces of the pie along with the end-of-the-year distributions. What they pass out now are problems. When things are like this, when people don't have money to buy, the first thing businesses cut is advertising. I'm getting older, too, Guido. The young, new copywriters are sweeping through. And they're hungry. These days they show up with professional degrees; advertising is a college major … You're going *where*?"

Esmé relented, accepted, detested. What could she do to stop him? She was so tired. The weight of responsibility made her lean over the table.

"The States. Evanston. A suburb of Chicago."

"And the papers? Are you going on a tourist visa? Are you planning to stay there illegally?"

Guido glanced at the door as if he were evaluating the possibilities of escape. Then he concentrated on stirring his coffee.

"Didn't Natalia ever tell you about my friend Shelly?"

"The Yanqui. One of them."

"I'm going on a fiancé visa. We're engaged. We're getting married there. Her lawyer told her it would be best that way; it's much easier to get a green card than if we marry here. I'll get my permanent residence right away, in a few months."

"So you're marrying up."

"In a way. If you want to look at it like that."

Esmé walked back home. She needed to tire herself out a little, to shake off the tingling that ran up and down her tension-seized muscles. There were lots of people sleeping in the street, a ridiculous number of shops with their blinds drawn and with "for sale" or "for rent" signs. Occasionally a horse-drawn wagon tied up the city traffic. She hadn't seen a horse-drawn wagon in the capital since she was a little girl. But Esmé wasn't paying attention to the signs of the crisis. She was thinking about the dead man, about his corpse and his covered face on the asphalt of the Costanera, about his wife and kids; she was thinking about the moment of impact, about that death for which she felt somehow guilty; she was thinking about her Natalia, her Natita, about the anguish she must be going through: although she hadn't been driving the car, she was there; she had felt the wheels run over him and then again in reverse (Esmé shuddered in horror for a moment), and now she had to live with that memory engraved in her, in her flesh, for the rest of her life.

She entered the apartment and went directly to her daughter's bedroom. She wouldn't wake her if she was asleep, but she needed to see her.

Natalia was just waking up. Her cheeks were rosy, one more than the other, from contact with the pillow. Her long, dark ringlets were tangled around her dear face. Fresh from sleep, she looked like a ten-year-old child; it would take her a few hours to assume the disdainful moue of adolescence. She leaped out of bed and ran over to hug her mother.

Esmé wasn't all that observant, but she couldn't help noticing that the shelf over the bed, where Natalia had displayed her dolls, the last vestige of her childhood, had been emptied and now held only a large, pale stone with a strange, smooth shape. Natalia followed her gaze.

"It's a piece of the barricade from the Costanera, Mamá. I took it as a souvenir."

Journal Entry 21

Natalia has just been re-baptized for the fourth time. At first she was called Paula. My daughters criticized the choice: they thought it was an unlikely name for someone her age. Suddenly I recalled that Paula was the name of Isabel Allende's daughter and also of the novel she dedicated to her after her death. It was impossible to use that name. For a little while it became Candela, but something indefinable bothered me about that over-the-top name. Esmé would never have called her daughter Candela. For a few months it became Luciana, but I rejected that as too trendy. A character's name should be special enough to be memorable without sounding strange or ridiculous, unless that strangeness serves a purpose in the story.

Natalia doesn't speak much; we hardly get to know her. In the end we have only her mother's vision of her. I know you as if I had given birth to you, a popular saying goes, but it's wrong. No one knows a person less than their own mother. Linguists maintain that prevarication, that is, the possibility of lying, is a unique, defining characteristic of human language. Many animals (gorillas, bees) communicate in diverse ways, but it's never been demonstrated that they're capable of lying. We humans lie to everyone we talk to, in addition to lying to ourselves with our inner voice. But nobody is lied to as much as one's own mother, even as she takes pleasure in confirming what she thinks she knows about her kids. She is the first woman a man – or a woman – lies to.

And another doubt. Writing is not for obsessives. It's like battling the thousand-headed Hydra: for every resolved doubt, two more pop up. You've got to write like Heracles, with a torch in your hand, cauterize the slit throats, keep on going somehow. The doubt: what kind of language to use? Should Naty use teenage slang? The slang of her day, which isn't exactly today's? Adolescent slang is so ephemeral … On the other hand, doesn't giving her a neutral, nondescript vocabulary detract from the story's realism? I'm reminded of the dilemma faced by John Cleland, the author of *Fanny Hill*, over the most appropriate language for narrating an erotic scene, doubts he expresses with such precision through his protagonist, the author of the letters that make up the novel. How to name the organs in conflict? How to describe the characters' actions? Is it better to choose scientific language, poetic language, streetspeak?

Borges, adopting a theoretical approach, always comes out against the jargon of the times. His own *Chronicles of Bustos Domecq*, written in collaboration with Adolfo Bioy Casares, provides evidence of how right he was: so old now that they sometimes seem incomprehensible, these chronicles make fun of expressions of which now barely a memory remains. Even *El Aleph* suffers from Carlos Argentino Daneri's rhetoric, no doubt hilarious in its day, but today divorced from any reference point whatsoever.

About my sources: To write this chapter I spoke with two lawyers and a judge.

G. is an attorney (not in criminal law) as well as a writer. He understood my problem perfectly and collaborated in the construction of the story. He was as anxious as I was to set up the scene of the accident and decide on the conduct of my characters. His enthusiasm was very helpful. By talking with him I realized that unintentional, as opposed to intentional, manslaughter, carried too light a penalty to justify Natalia's putting the blame on Rita. And I needed for everything to be more serious, for Naty to worm her way out of a fairly serious sentence and manage to discharge it on her (former) friend.

The judge I spoke to had also been a criminal lawyer. I didn't know him; I found him through a mutual friend, and he welcomed me with enormous kindness and an absolute lack of interest in my problem. During our conversation it became clear that he found the deed my characters were involved in quite trivial, that anyone could resolve it, that it was a matter almost unworthy of his rank. Something like using a nuclear reactor to make a couple of fried eggs. He got lost in digressions concerning much more complicated, more serious, more interesting cases, and it was hard for me to steer him back on track. And yet his disdain turned out to be very useful in helping me understand that I needed to include aggravating circumstances. He was the one who told me about gross negligence, citing the Cabello case (a boy who killed two people, possibly while drag racing) and praised the precision of the gendarmerie's scopometrical instruments.

And finally I talked to Z., a young, very interesting criminal lawyer with an active practice, who was quite familiar with the relationship with the police and who explained to me what the laws say and how they really work, what hit-and-run consists of, what factors could aggravate my characters' situation. It was he who explained to me that he preferred the word "advisees" to "clients."

The Trial

The trial was long, slow, grueling. Much more like Dr. Mertens' threats than like Dr. Martegut's gesture of sweeping crumbs off the tablecloth. And after all, is sweeping crumbs off the tablecloth really that simple? Isn't it nearly impossible, a task for which different instruments have been invented and which can be achieved only by taking the tablecloth off the table and shaking it?

The toxicology reports proved that the two girls had used alcohol and Ecstasy that night, that they had smoked marijuana, and that neither of them was in any condition to drive. Fingerprints from both of them were on the steering wheel. Esmé mortgaged the apartment in order to get Natalia the best defense possible, and she did. Several young witnesses testified that Rita often drove Natalia's car, or rather, Natalia's mother's car. It was even possible to get two very important witnesses to testify in the case, the man who watched the cars that were parked outside the club's parking lot, and a neighbor who at that moment was standing in the doorway of his house. Both of them affirmed that they had seen Rita get behind the wheel of the Golf when they came out of the disco. Esmé never asked her lawyers how they had managed to secure those testimonies, so useful and so necessary. The owner of the *choripán* and *bondiola* stand changed his statement:

now that he had a chance to look at both of them carefully, he realized that he could, indeed, recognize the girl driving the car. It was Rita, without a doubt.

But equally important were the sincerity and energy with which Naty fought to defend her friend at various points in the trial. After breaking down during cross-examination by the D.A., she could no longer declare herself guilty. It was easy to see, then, how painfully, how reluctantly, she recognized Rita's guilt, and how she tried to minimize it by giving all sorts of contradictory explanations. Rita, in turn, with her incoherent tale, made a very bad impression on the D.A. and the investigating judge. When she spoke more clearly, it was even worse. At times it seemed obvious that she was repeating by rote (Rita never was a very good student) what her lawyer had tried to make her remember. Each time she spoke, she used the very same words. On the other hand, when Natalia was questioned face-to-face, her personality, her clarity and personal charm, her obvious shyness, her efforts to cause the least possible harm to her friend despite considering her guilty, her brief attempt to take the blame once more, made her testimony seem much more credible than the brutal slurs that the out-of-control Rita hurled at her former friend. Even Dr. Mertens (and that really *was* an exceptional achievement) ended up being convinced that she was defending an innocent girl. And proving that innocence was very important, because the situation was becoming more complicated, since the charge was no longer involuntary manslaughter, which would have gotten her a suspended sentence. Instead, the D.A. insisted on gross negligence, a powerful argument that evoked a famous case.

On August 30, 1999, Sebastián Cabello, then 19 years old, was driving along Avenida Cantilo in his Honda Civic, when he rammed into the back of a Renault in which Celia González, a 39-year-old veterinarian and her three-year-old daughter, Vanina, were traveling. As a result of the tremendous impact, the vehicle in which the victims were riding was thrust 92 meters forward in a straight line and immediately burst into flames. Mother and daughter died in the blaze. Forensic investigation revealed that Cabello, who was accompanied by a friend, was driving at a speed of 85.5 miles per hour, apparently in a drag race with a black BMW.

The accident was widely covered by the media, and Cabello was remanded into pre-trial custody. The husband/father of the victims, overcome with emotion, beat Cabello as he was being led to trial, handcuffed. On advice from legal counsel, the young man refrained from bringing suit against his aggressor, declaring through spokespersons that he understood the father's reaction and his pain.

In 2003 the Oral Criminal Court, in a fairly unusual judgment, sentenced Cabello to twelve years in prison, finding him criminally responsible on two counts of voluntary manslaughter with conditional intent.

Two years later, Chamber III of the Criminal Appeals Court, maintaining that the drag race allegations had not been proved, was to reclassify the crime, reducing the sentence to three years, suspended. But at the time Rita and Natalia's case was going on, the result of the appeal was still unforeseeable and Cabello was in prison.

From Evanston, Illinois, Guido contacted his daughter, first through MSN and then by Skype. Guido's ability to master the latest technology had always irritated Esmé. It struck her as inappropriate for someone of their generation always to be the first to use it. The famous Green Card was in process, but not imminent. For the moment it was impossible for him to send money. He didn't have a job, but Shelly was doing very well, and as usual, he had plans, lots of extraordinary plans. When he was able to carry one of them out – just one! – and especially when that stupid, ridiculous, pointless case was over, which didn't allow him go see his daughter, he would take Naty with him, he promised, he threatened. He'd pay for her to attend a good college in the United States, the promised land. Sometimes Guido would also talk to his ex-wife, to ask her opinion about how the trial was going. No matter how much Esmé forbade herself to do it, no matter how she tried to avoid it, all the conversations with her ex ended up with her asking for money, a useless argument, repeated a thousand times. Most of the time Guido would hang up abruptly in mid-sentence.

More than ever before, Esmé needed to be near her mother. After reaching seventy-something, Alcira had developed a kind of turkey wattle, wrinkled and trembling, between her neck and chin. Esmé never was able to accept that new body part on her mother, a woman who had always been so perfect, so strong, so upright. It was an inconceivable bit of untidiness that caused Esmé as much anguish as the age spots on Alcira's hands.

Now they were in Alcira's kitchen, and it wasn't easy to get her in there. She had always preferred the dining room: the embroidered tablecloth, the good china, the bakery-bought pastries, the programmed visits. For generational reasons, Esmé felt more comfortable in the kitchen, the warmest spot in the house. They were drinking *mate* and spreading non-fat white cheese on thin slices of toast. Alcira meticulously picked up every crumb that fell to the sides of the plate.

"How many times have I asked you to eat *over* the plate?" she asked Esmé with a little smile.

"How many times in my life? One million two hundred and forty-nine thousand?"

"And look what I accomplished …"

"Mamá. Do you really think Rita was driving the car?"

"Daughter, you're very sick in the head. What difference does it make who was driving the car? There's just one question you need to ask. Who's your daughter. Period. Is Rita your daughter?"

"What would Regina have said, Mamá? You know how I admired her. For me, she was … We never talk about Regina. She was the one who knew if something was all right or not. Whenever I had doubts, I looked at her; I looked at her face. She knew."

"We don't talk because there's nothing to talk about."

"She was … She did what she thought needed to be done. To the end. You admired her too, Mamá. You and Papá. And you can't say her name because you still love her. Regina was your favorite; don't tell me she wasn't."

"You don't understand anything. Regina was an idiot who let herself get killed. I hate her."

Alcira's face started to shrink and wrinkle up as if the

turkey wattle had somehow taken over all her skin, all her features, turning them into something soft, moist, and repulsive, made of stifled sobs.

"She was so young, Esmé … Don't think she was better. She was just young, demanding, a fundamentalist. Later on she would have been like you, like me, like everyone. She was so young when they killed her … She didn't have time to hunker down, to give up, to lie, to fool herself, to grow. She didn't have time for anything, she didn't have an ever after, she never grew up. And I forced her to wear braces for so many years!"

Rita was convicted of manslaughter. The court accepted the verdict of guilty on the charge of gross negligence, and the girl, who at the time was over eighteen, served almost a year in jail, while her lawyers appealed the sentence. Natalia was absolved of guilt and all charges.

Journal Entry 22

I take up writing the novel again after a month of hiatus, of rest. It's astonishing how infinitely slowly I'm building the story. It's the fault of a couple of short story books that have turned my head around. *Suddenly a Knock on the Door* by Etgar Keret, an Israeli writer, an extravagance of controlled madness, of brilliant, delirious ideas that nonetheless don't take the characters away from their daily lives, their problems: so recognizable, so widely shared. And *Animales domésticos* by Chilean author Alejandra Costamagna, which demonstrates that the short story is a renewable genre, despite what many people may say. Costamagna's prose elides certain things, skips over others, joins others together, in a highly original way, demonstrating and displaying this world's new sensibility, a little mysterious for my generation, a world that excludes me, one that I can no longer understand very well.

It's remarkable how the feeling of verisimilitude grows when I describe the Cabello case. The precision of the data makes everything much more believable. Those involved come bearing first and last names, ages, and occupations. The exact date of the events is mentioned, the speed at which the car was traveling, the distance the other vehicle was moved. When it comes time to make people believe something, numbers are far more effective than letters.

But I don't want to make anyone believe anything, right? If I were putting all my money on verisimilitude, this journal would make no sense.

Natalia Grows Up

Natalia finished high school by the skin of her teeth. Earning her diploma took her more or less the same amount of time as the trial. At the end of her fifth year, when she joined her classmates on the graduation trip, she still had six subjects to test out of, and it seemed logical that it would be hard for her to concentrate under so much pressure. Over the next two years, she passed the exams little by little.

After the Unfortunate Accident, the school principal acted more understanding than anyone had expected: the year was almost over and soon she'd be rid of the two undesirables forever, in the smoothest possible way, less disturbing for the other parents. In a meeting with Esmé, she never stopped referring to the occurrence with those words that defined and assuaged it: the Unfortunate Accident. Among their schoolmates, the Unfortunate Accident conferred a strange prestige on Natalia and Rita; they were treated with respect.

The club where the graduation party was held required the participation of at least four adults. Esmé refused to be one of them and was happy she did. As the parents had promised the disco owners they would control alcohol consumption (beer only for those over eighteen, no hard liquor, no more than two drinks apiece), the kids methodically got drunk beforehand and arrived at the party in a regrettable state. Natalia, who now carefully controlled her alcohol intake, was just a little tipsy, but Rita, disgustingly, pathetically drunk, attacked her in the middle of the party, threatening to kill her. Bigmouth slut, fucking murderer, she said, I'm gonna shove your lies up your ass, I'm gonna punch your tits off, I'm gonna trash your cunt with smallpox, she said, declared those who witnessed the encounter. Natalia responded by tossing her beer into Rita's face, glass included. The classmates, whose opinions on the matter were still divided (with a small majority favoring Natalia) required nothing more to unleash the urge to fight, hit, and destroy, a common response to alcohol in the very young. The party ended in a collective brawl worthy of a Wild West saloon, which the caretakers of the disco managed to subdue only with great effort and following considerable damage to the place. The parents helped out as best they could, trying to rescue or restrain their children.

While the trial was going on, it was very important for Natalia's conduct to be impeccable. Above all, it was essential for her not to commit any act that would require police intervention. Esmé wondered whether or not she should let her participate in the graduation trip to Bariloche, an initiation rite that was frenetic and sad at the same time, organized by businesses dedicated primarily to extracting the maximum amount of money possible from the parents. She attended an initial meeting with the representative of one of the firms they consulted, a very young guy who would also act as group coordinator. More than anything else, she was shocked by the boy's expert sales ability in convincing both the parents and the children that they were planning a unique, different experience, especially tailored to the interests of that very special group, while he signed them up for the one and only trip, obviously the same for everyone, that they really offered.

Drugs, alcohol, and uncontrolled sex were the parents' fears and the children's desire. The businesses couldn't have cared less, just as long as they didn't have problems with the police. A friend whose daughter had already been on the famous Bariloche trip told Esmé that a few kilometers before the bus passed through a police checkpoint, the coordinator had made the kids hand over all the drugs and booze they were carrying, promising to return them later, at the hotel.

When she discussed the subject with Natalia, convinced at this point that she shouldn't go on this trip and determined to wage a long, difficult battle, Esmé's daughter surprised her, using vulgar language that she didn't normally employ with her parents. Even in this regard her adolescence was quite different: as a girl, Esmé had flaunted street talk, those words that were not allowed in her house, incorporating them eagerly into her language every day and shocking Alcira and León. Natalia, on the other hand, spoke to her parents in calm, reassuring, neutral language, very different from what she used with people her own age. (Esmé was sometimes taken aback when she heard Naty talking on the phone). That was why Natalia's refusal to participate in the graduation party took her by surprise, not only in content, but in form.

"I'm not going, Mamá. I'm into other stuff. There are people who need the graduation trip to get hammered, high, and fuck one another blind. It doesn't interest me."

What did Natalia mean? That she got high and hammered without the need for an excuse? (Esmé refused to include sex in the realm of her worries).

Even though she wanted to know as little as possible about the dead man's family, even though she refused to become familiar with his face, his story, his life, it was impossible to avoid. The man had been divorced and was remarried to a younger woman. He had two small children, ages five and seven, and an 18-year-old from his first wife, who brutally attacked Rita coming out of a hearing. The three children and the second wife were the plaintiffs. The woman refused to talk to the press. She simply cried at all the courtroom sessions she attended. Her financial situation was very precarious; her attorney had agreed to collect after the civil trial, when the insurance paid off.

"Poor people," said Esmé, crestfallen. They were having coffee near the Tribunales neighborhood.

"Poor, poor people! How horrible!" Natalia raised the stakes. "And poor Rita, too, Mamá. I don't know how I'd feel if I were responsible for something like that."

Esmé stared at her hard, and Naty stared right back with her eternally limpid eyes, always clear, always focused. Suddenly her expression disintegrated into a expression of hatred.

"You don't believe me, do you? As usual! Everyone but you believes me. My classmates, the court, people. Even the dead man's family realizes I'm innocent! But you always have to think the worst of me.

"I didn't say anything."

"But we know each other."

"We know each other?"

"I don't know. Did you notice that I'm in love?"

With one of her best smiles and the promise of a woman-to-woman chat, Natalia had turned the conversation around. In love? At the time Dr. Martegut had suggested that having a stable partner was something that always made a good impression at a trial.

But aside from that, was Natalia's accusation completely false? Wasn't she right? Didn't it even explain that disgusting idea that had just crossed her mind about her daughter's supposed love? And Esmé wondered if it wasn't, in fact, true that the cruel nip of doubt had always, Naty's whole life long, troubled her relationship with her daughter? Wasn't it true that many times she had struggled to silence a certain lack of confidence, of suspicion? Did all mothers get that feeling, or was it just her, Esmé wondered, that horrid idea that her daughter was lying to her, or holding back part of the truth, just as all children do with all parents, just as she had done with Alcira, but more and worse, because now she was the mother, the one responsible, the guilty party, the one who had shaped that clay that could have turned out to be a work of art, but perhaps was not. And wasn't any small deviation, any minuscule error that diverged from the ideal, her own fault, completely hers? Hadn't that shadow of doubt, of fear, that inability to believe in her daughter completely, blindly, totally, to believe in her words, her possibilities, her illusions, her accomplishments, been what caused the divergence? Wasn't she, with her lack of confidence, her suspicions, the one who had caused those very imperfections she rejected as if they weren't her own creation, her product, the result of her own imperfect actions and thoughts?

Now Esmé carried a weight in her heart, more than a dead weight, a living monster that was eating away at her from within. How could she free herself of that horror, how could she believe Naty's words again, have confidence in her gaze? Whom could she talk to? Not to Alcira, who got along perfectly with her granddaughter, for better or for worse. Not to her friends: speaking ill of one's children was like spitting at heaven.

Natalia's boyfriend was Lautaro, and Esmé wasn't as surprised as she would have liked to be, but she dissembled adequately.

"But I thought you hated him! Wasn't he the one who told Pippi Wrongstocking that you were a dealer?"

"Well, I'm older now, Mamá. We ran into one another again at a club, and you should have seen him apologize. Pathetic. It made me feel sorry for him."

"Darling, pity isn't a good basis for forming a relationship."

"But I love him, too, Mamá. How could I not love him? He's such a sweetie. He'd do anything for me."

In point of fact, Lautaro was prepared to do anything for Natalia, and it was pathetic to see him drag himself before her like a puppy, with his tongue always hanging out, desperate to earn a glance, a caress, a gesture of approval. Lautaro's parents hadn't forgotten the shady reasons why their son had changed schools. Natalia wasn't welcome at their house. But they didn't dare close the door in her face, either.

The boy's mother wanted to get together with Esmé one afternoon. Lautaro was already in his second year of Biology and was a T.A. in one subject. Now he had given up a graduate scholarship to complete his studies at The Hague. A once-in-a-lifetime opportunity, his mother emphasized.

"He didn't want to be away from Natalia," she said gravely.

"It's their life … And once-in-a-lifetime opportunities don't exist. Just like this one came along, something else will come along for him – he's such an intelligent boy. And besides, what can I do? What can we do?"

"I'm not asking you to do anything. I'd just like to know if your daughter loves him. If she really loves him. If she would be willing to give up something for him. Whatever it might be. Because Natalia doesn't give up anything, I'd say. She's stood him up more than once. Lautaro doesn't know what she does, where she goes, or with whom. He's going crazy."

"Was that all we had to talk about?" Esmé cut her off.

"I also wanted to ask you if you and your ex are the ones giving her so much money. Because that girl handles a lot of money, Esmeralda. I can't accuse her of living off Lautaro – we've got him on a very short leash."

Esmé paid for the coffees, got up, and left.

She hated those mothers (especially mothers of sons) who insisted on showing how bad influences, girlfriends, or the wrong friends, were responsible for everything that happened in life. For everything they didn't like or weren't prepared to admire in their own children.

Meanwhile, there was one more step that the lawyers considered necessary: Natalia needed to undergo psychological treatment. Esmé agreed, of course. The great, universal remedy for Argentines was set in motion yet again.

Esmé consulted several therapists, immediately rejecting those who used the expression "promiscuous adolescent", which they certainly would never have used with a male. This time the chosen therapist was a man, Dr. Roth. Natalia accepted him without argument and tolerated him agreeably for the length of the trial. Esmé had a couple of conversations with the doctor, who seemed delighted with his patient's progress. In fact, ever since the Unfortunate Accident (by now everyone close to Natalia had begun referring to it that way), Natalia hadn't gotten drunk again or appeared to be smoking marijuana. If it was a question of believing in influences, Lautaro perhaps was one of the good ones.

As soon as the trial was over, Natalia simultaneously ended both her relationship and her psychological treatment.

JOURNAL ENTRY 23

Today we mothers are those monsters who are constantly accused of filicide, or at the very least, of marking our children's destiny with indelible, destructive strokes. Middle-class mothers, especially, those of us who don't even have the excuse of poverty and abandonment, mothers with husbands and household help, mothers who are obliged to control every one of our words and gestures, because everything leaves its traces on that apparently malleable clay known as our children's conscience. In other words, we're the ones who are guilty of everything.

With one small loophole: we have been daughters, too. Our own mothers, therefore, are largely responsible for our shameful current condition. Modern psychology offers us the possibility of sharing the responsibility with our parents and blaming them for our problems, just as tomorrow we will be blamed for the anxieties of our descendants. Parents shall guiltily bear their children's guilt unto the third and fourth generations. Thus, the question of fatalism versus free will has shifted from religion to psychoanalysis. It isn't that poor little thing's fault, people say: what else can you expect with a mother like that.

Not long ago I allowed myself the pleasure of rereading a book that was very popular during my childhood: *Heart* by Edmondo de Amicis. And once again I confirmed how the concepts that have ruled our lives since the beginning of the 15th century have changed. At that time, no one would ever believe that a mother could be responsible in any way for her offspring's misdeeds. A mother was generous, self-sacrificing, infinitely good, just by virtue of being a MOTHER. A mother never made mistakes and always did what was best for her child. A child was bad because he had been born that way, as an effect of the perversity that flowed in his blood, plus his own will to be evil.

The narrator of *Heart* describes the evils of a perverse friend in a way that is crystal clear. He is the wicked Franti, who at age nine beats up all the other kid, challenges his teachers, and gets bad grades in every subject. Franti's father is a criminal and is in jail. No one considers that the circumstances in which Franti was raised might have some connection to his wickedness: he is the way he is because he wants to be. Instead of blaming the mother for God-knows-what terrible mistakes she's made in the child's upbringing, instead of suggesting she visit an educational psychologist's office, the teacher, in an unforgettable scene, grabs Franti by the arm, makes him face that poor woman who places a twisted hand on her heart, and says to him: "Franti, you're killing your mother!"

On the other hand, it concerns me that Natalia might be seen as a model for her generation. There's nothing worse than prototypical, symbolic characters. The fact that so many generational clichés appear in the text (the graduation trip, the alcohol consumption) forces me to constantly skirt that danger. But at the same time, they're unavoidable, landmarks in the lives of teenagers of the third millennium. Natalia should be seen as *sui generis* and not as a model or prototype. It's essential to avoid at all costs those dyads like: good-committed-socially conscious generation vs. irresponsible-indifferent-uncommitted-egotistical-individualistic generation. Besides, I don't believe in them.

Earlier this week I was discussing this book with my agent. I think that once you cross the 200-page mark, there's no turning back: this is going to be a novel, and therefore I can start talking about it (but just a little).

N... isn't so sure about my Journal: Won't it get in the way of the reading itself? Couldn't it disconcert the reader, affecting the credibility of the story? Maybe, to an extent. But one writes what one would like to read. And as a reader, even if I weren't part of the profession, I would love to have the writer tell me where she got her materials from, how she chose to put them all together, what choices she made, and what doubts she has.

THE REENCOUNTER

Esmé struggles to find a relatively comfortable sleeping position in the airplane seat, which constrains her miserably. Her purse and laptop take up a good portion of the sad, limited space reserved for her feet. The upper portion of the backrest has something resembling lapels that can be expanded to support her head. That is, they would, if she were only ten centimeters bigger. She can't control the movement of her legs, which cross and uncross, desperately trying to find a place where they can rest. She nods off, her head supported by her hands and her elbow on the armrest, but she's immediately awakened by numbness in her arm, followed by pins and needles. She tries to tip the seat back a little more, but it's impossible: the seatback's range of motion is limited, almost symbolic. However, it's enough to allow the seat in front of her to practically dig into her face. Her living space becomes even smaller; even breathing feels difficult. As she becomes more alert, she's engulfed by a heat wave that comes from within, forcing her to peel away from the perspiration-soaked seatback. It's obvious she won't be able to fall asleep again. Better, then, to try to concentrate on the film they're showing on those screens that are suspended from the ceiling in the aisle. It's not one of those new planes with screens on the seat in front. She puts on the headphones and finds the

Spanish language channel. She knows the sound is poor, and in English she won't understand a word. She doesn't understand a word in Spanish, either. Sitting next to her is a strangely elegant woman, dressed in a well-tailored suit, some kind of high-ranking office worker who even at the airport stood out among the crowd of travelers in sneakers, comfortable pants, and baggy tee shirts. Esmé takes a deep breath, emitting a sound that resembles a groan. Her traveling companion latches on to that sigh.

"At least you can travel comfortably," she says to Esmé. "As soon as I get there, they take me directly to the company." It's obvious that she needs to justify her attire.

"I'm going to visit my daughter, who's studying at the University of Virginia. She's not expecting me. I'm going to surprise her!" And she wished her traveling companion knew, without her needing to say so, that the University of Virginia was considered to be one of the twenty best universities in the U.S. If only it were Harvard or Yale, she wouldn't need to explain.

Esmé would have liked to provide her with more details, to tell her that the girl, so young, isn't all alone in a foreign country, that she's not *that* kind of mother, that her daughter's father lives in Chicago, far away, true, but at least he's in the same hemisphere, in the same country, in that half of the continent that North Americans call America. That her father invited her to live with him, and that after just a few months, their daughter applied to and was accepted by the University of Virginia, that it was her ex who finally decided to foot the bill for something important, and that she only hopes that the money will last till Natalia finishes college, that he was always so unpredictable – or maybe so predictable – but anyway, she's becoming entangled in thoughts that she'll never be able to tell her traveling companion; on the other hand, she would like to tell her that her daughter Natalia is perfectly fluent in English because she went to bilingual schools all her life and that she's very, *very* intelligent, all grown up now, capable of figuring out that certain universities need to fill an international student quota, capable of doing community work or actively participating in politically correct groups in order to earn the additional points to compensate for her mediocre high school grades. Or maybe there's no reason to give out so much information, and really she doesn't have to, because her traveling companion politely asks her to let her out to go to the bathroom, the only reason she's taken off her headphones, and when she returns she pops them back on again, with a pleasant smile, almost an apology, and becomes engrossed in the movie. Esmé watches the soundless images for a while, but they strike her as completely phony, unrealistic, pure cinematographic artifice, and yet she knows that if she could understand what the characters were saying, she'd be able to forget everything, believe in the story unquestioningly, get swept away by the plot with the same passion as the other passengers, motionless in their seats, whose only sign of life is the movement of their eyes.

In Atlanta she has two hours to change terminals and find the connecting flight to Charlottesville, where the university is located. It's not the first time she's traveled to the U.S., and she breathes deeply in order to blend in with that special smell, that terribly *Yanqui* smell airports have, a mixture of cinnamon, pizza, plastic, glue, and de-odorant. As she runs unnecessarily (there's plenty of time) through the airport, she tries to picture her daughter's face. They're in touch frequently; they see one another on screen, exchange photos and videos, but it's been over a year, more than a whole year since she's seen her, and photos don't tell all. It's been so long since Natalia's sent a full-length photo, and her face looks fuller. Esmé worries that she's put on weight from fast food, from the excessive availability of food that spills out all over the map of the United States.

She boards the connecting flight, thinking for the thousandth time that maybe she's made a mistake, that it would be so nice to get off the plane and find Natalia wait-ing for her, that maybe it wasn't such a good idea to show up this way, unannounced. During the brief flight between Atlanta and Charlottesville, her legs settle down, she relaxes (she's almost there), and at last she falls deeply asleep.

A taxi takes her from the airport to her daughter's address, the address that she's caressed so many times on the packages she's mailed her. Natalia asked for silly, sweet things associated with her childhood, things that touched her. Old but well-loved clothing, the fuchsia nightgown, now in tatters, the glass clown her grandmother had giv-en her, the cup shaped like a squirrel. Come visit me, Na-talia always said, come whenever you want, but whenever you want wasn't so easy. Esmé was living in a wartime economy, working part-time at an advertising agency and supplementing her salary with free-lance jobs that were harder and harder to find and which paid less and less. Alcira had become a domineering old woman, still sturdy and in command, but weaker, always difficult, ready to fire maids and/or nurses without a shred of mercy for her daughter, who had to fill in with her body and her life every time one of the caregivers called her to say she was quitting. In the past year Alcira had a fall that resulted in two herniated disks and a bout of pneumonia that sent her to the hospital for two weeks, although by now she was nearly all better. It wasn't a simple matter for Esmé to leave her alone in the city. Her mother's friends were old, too, more or less invalids, and they hardly ever visited.

The taxi driver is black, very black, far from the *café con leche* shade of most North American blacks, and he is eager for conversation. Esmé discovers, to her surprise, that she understands nearly everything he says. Her English comprehension is hit-or-miss; she's been practicing a little with the T.V., but she can never quite manage to understand all the news on CNN. Whenever she loses the gist or isn't familiar with the topic, there's no way she can pick up the thread again. They ride along, chatting constantly, like Argentines. The taxi driver tells her that he's Senegalese, which explains his lovely foreign accent, and that he's lived in Charlottesville for five years. Esmé discovers that New York isn't the only cosmopolitan city, that in the U.S. immigrants from around the world spill over everywhere.

They reach her daughter's address. The neighborhood and modest, ground-floor apartment, part of a complex, seem almost familiar. Natalia has sent her many photos. She begged her father for permission to live away from campus, where only the youngest students lived. Only the best, those with the highest graders, occupy those ancient rooms, designed by Jefferson, without private bathrooms, an unknown luxury in the 19ᵗʰ century, dorms with shared baths and showers, identifiable by their piles of firewood in the doorway, because they have no central heating, either. But Natalia is twenty, older than most of her freshman classmates, and she preferred renting a tiny apartment in town with a friend, an arrangement that was no more expensive than living on campus.

Esmé knows that showing up unannounced has consequences, and she prepares herself for this eventuality. If her daughter isn't at home, she'll decamp to a nearby Starbucks, which she's already located on the map. She has very little luggage, just her carry-on and a purse. And she'll phone from there. What luck for Natalia, what luck for everyone that Guido was able to offer her that possibility of starting over in a different country, in another world, after everything she's gone through, poor thing.

No matter how she tries to prepare herself for not finding her at home, for knocking pointlessly at the door, Esmé feels her heart race as she stands at the threshold of that new, independent, world, which her daughter no longer shares with her. And yet she can hear noises, footsteps; the door opens. Natalia is there, staring at her, slack-jawed, her eyes widened in surprise, her face, in fact, fuller, and carrying a six or seven-month pregnancy. She's wearing jogging pants that cling to her belly and a loose, dark blue tee shirt that says "I'm not fat, I'm pregnant."

Esmé's soul melts; love rushes desperately through her veins and climbs to her eyes. She hugs her as if she never wants to let her go. Natalia returns the embrace affectionately, but with less emotion.

"Mamá! What are you doing here?" Natalia smiles. What luck, what a relief: Esmé had been so afraid of her disapproving expression, her ill humor, the sour remark that would punish her for showing up like that, without advance warning.

"*Hijita*, my love, my darling, you didn't say anything, why didn't you tell me anything? Do you think I … Don't you know me? Are you alone, sweetheart, my baby. Does it have a daddy? Does Guido know?" Esmé rubbed her daughter's belly. She couldn't take her hand off that belly.

"No, he doesn't know. We saw each other a couple of months ago, but I wasn't showing yet. But yes, Mamá, of course it has a daddy. You'll meet him soon."

"But why, why didn't you tell me … I never imagined …"

"Ha, ha, look who's talking! I never imagined I'd suddenly see you here. Come on in, I'll get you settled, and we'll have a nice cup of tea."

Esmé enters a strange state of suspense; an electrical charge runs up and down her skin. She no longer feels fatigue, those waves of exhaustion that always knock her out after spending the night on a plane. Now she's not thinking about going to bed or resting; she's thinking only of all the things they have to tell one another, those terrible, wonderful words that she's about to exchange with her daughter, about the grandchild growing in his warm, safe nest.

"Do you know if it's a boy or a girl?"

"A little boy, of course. His name is Timothy."

"A *Yanqui* name? Then the father is from here?"

"The father and the mother."

"But you're the mother!"

"Well … not exactly. You see, there's a contract … Mamá, you'll have grandchildren someday, I promise, but not this one, okay? This one isn't your grandchild." Natalia speaks calmly, enunciating the words in order to achieve the greatest possible understanding of what she's saying.

"A contract?" Esmé repeats, idiotically.

And then, suddenly, she understands. And with that comprehension, a cold wave passes through her body, which until now had been wrapped in a grandmother's velvety warmth. A frozen blast, loaded with ice crystals, lodges in the interstices of her heart and from there blows toward the rest of her body. Her fingers grow cold; she can't feel her feet.

"Natalia … I don't understand. *Hijita*, why …"

"For money, Mamá. I needed money."

"Money! But I would've given you money … your father …"

"A hundred thousand dollars?"

"Why do you need a hundred thousand dollars?"

"See? You and Papi could never have given me that money. But even if you could have, look, you haven't given me anything, and already you're starting in with the questions. I need freedom, Mamá. And freedom comes from money with no strings attached. I'm going to get into a very interesting business and I needed capital. And I don't want to talk about that."

"But you're … a foreigner! … You can't sign a contract!" You sold your womb!"

"I didn't sell anything, Mamá. I rented it out. It's a renewable resource. And I did sign a contract, because now I'm Puerto Rican and I'm twenty-four years old."

"You're walking around with fake documents? You're in the United States, at the university, with fake documents?"

"I'm not at the university, Mamá. I was planning to talk to Papá after this is over. And don't jump to the wrong conclusions: the documents aren't fake; they're absolutely authentic. A Puerto Rican girl sold them to me, and I paid for them as if they were real – and they are."

"But you …"

"The only problem was that I was stopped for a traffic violation and a record of tickets came up that I wasn't expecting. Now I have to take a class so I can keep using the registration. And you can't be here without car registration, you know, a car is life."

"But the parents …"

"The parents are coming over this afternoon. You can stay if you want; they're nice people. They'll be thrilled to meet my mom. You don't even have to fake a Puerto Rican accent. They can't tell the difference."

Esmé is sitting on a chair that's slightly too low for her knees, which will start to protest after a while in that position. She picks up her teacup, which has no handle, and burns her hand, but she's almost grateful for the pain that momentarily distracts her from her anguish and reminds her that she has a body.

Looking around, she now understands in a different way the neutrality she had noticed when she walked into her daughter's apartment. The Japanese landscape engravings on the wall, the impeccable carpet, the sound system, the computer …

"And what about college? Aren't you planning to go back to college anymore? Next year?" she asked, crestfallen because she already knows the answer.

Idiot, she says to herself. Under these horrible circumstances, why are you making such a big deal of something so silly, so unimportant? But if she were studying, at least, if at least she kept up with her studies … Like most parents, including those of her generation, Esmé imbues the university with indisputable, magical qualities.

"Think of all the money I'm saving you guys, Mamá. And I say you guys, plural, because you know as well as I do that Papá isn't going to keep paying by himself. He's already late with payments. In the end you would have had to pitch in."

Esmé tries to think of money and money problems and the arguments with Guido that she won't have to face, but she can think only of the baby growing in her daughter's womb and of the mysterious venture involving one hundred thousand dollars, that bit of entrepreneurship that cannot be discussed. She's afraid, very afraid. The exertion of a sleepless night falls on her like a hairy, heavy, enormous bear. She thinks of ways to remain close to her grandson. She could report her, talk to a lawyer: signed with fake documents, that contract can't be legal. And her daughter would be deported, but that wouldn't be so bad: she could get her back. Or would she go to jail? Naty is in the USA on a student visa. She's not an illegal immigrant. Could she, then, go to jail? But the baby … how to get the baby back? There's the matter of DNA. The father would lay claim to the baby, anyway. Any maybe the mother, the other one … But, besides, who is the real mother? Could Natalia be the real mother, the owner of the egg, the womb? Or just the womb? Couldn't the mother also be a third party, an anonymous egg donor? Whom did the egg belong to? Whose sperm were they? Did they belong to the guy they had bought them from? Because the embryo, even though it was no longer an embryo, almost seven months along now, the fetus, the fetus, the baby, it was perfectly clear whom he belonged to: he belonged to the one that paid, the one who had offered the contact. She doesn't have to force her mind to be still; an internal silence gradually takes over. She needs to change, unpack her suitcase, lie down in a bed, but it's better like this, it's better to escape from this confusing, painful world, to escape; sleep carries her along a dark, peaceful trail, and it's better like this, to let herself gently slip onto the sofa, to fall asleep effortlessly, without unfastening her bra, grateful to be wearing an old, comfortable, elastic-waist pair of pants, to sink mindlessly into a dreamless sleep from which she's awakened by the cruel ringing of the doorbell.

"It's the parents," Naty says.

"But I wanted to change, brush my teeth …" Suddenly she realizes that she wants to make a good impression, to assert herself with a certain presence before those strangers who are coming to steal from her, to become for one moment a severe, tall, elegant woman.

"You're just fine as you are, Mamá." Naty makes the international sign for silence before opening the door, and Esmé understands that it suits her daughter's purposes to introduce a slightly disheveled mother, dressed in old clothes, with red eyes and bad breath. Something more similar to the cliché of a Puerto Rican mother whose daughter has made the hard, but necessary, decision to rent out her womb.

In walk the parents – the real parents of the baby Natalia is carrying in her body, the parents who have paid, or have committed to pay, for that baby. (What could the contract be like? Did it include advance deposits, graduated payments?). More than parents, they're the owners, and Esmé thinks that if this were a novel, if only it were a novel, what follows could be omitted. In a novel, in a film, there's no need to contend with the damn succession of seconds that make up each minute. It would be possible to skip the entire scene and go directly to another situation, take a leap in time and land a few months after birth, with Natalia already recovered, possibly back in school, at another university. Or the leap might be geographical: she might be in Buenos Aires. Natalia might not even show up in the next scene; Esmé might not show up. Nonetheless, she stands up to greet Mr. and Mrs. Dobbs politely. He's a short, brawny man, that ruddy blond type whose skin reddens with every change of mood. He greets her with kindness and a curious expression, but doesn't extend his hand. He doesn't want to touch her. Mrs. Dobbs, on the other hand, embraces her warmly. She has straight hair and dark skin, and she wears a sari, which she uses to identify with the culture of India, a country where she was not born, though her parents were, Natalia explains, those puzzled grandparents of the grandchild who, in two months, will be nestled in their arms.

Everything that happens after that develops as in a dream, like in one of those ridiculous dreams, not exactly a nightmare, though she can't help feeling an atmosphere of angst hovering over the scene; or maybe it's a lie – she's the only one who feels it; the others are happy, used to everything. The baby's parents seem to know the house quite well.

Mrs. Dobbs takes over in the kitchen. She's brought a chocolate cake and a paper bag filled with delights, which she neatly arranges, Italian and French cheeses, Alaskan salmon, Pepperidge Farms cinnamon cookies, which don't really go with the imported delicacies, but which Natalia loves, she explains to Esmé as if apologizing. Mr. Dobbs and his wife try in every possible way to be friendly and charming; they try to seduce her. The wife makes green tea for everyone. We'd rather she not drink coffee, she explains to the mother of the hydroponic tank where her son is growing. If only she *were* a machine, that woman must be thinking; if only she were a machine and not another human being, another unpredictable, damn human being, another woman, with desires, and lies, and not her daughter, thinks Esmé, too, but not Natalia. Who knows what Natalia is thinking: at the moment she appears infinitely comfortable and relaxed in her role. She eats a piece of cake, chats pleasantly with the owners of the baby, who is moving around in her belly. She takes the mother's hand and places it on that belly so she can feel the energetic kicks of that thing they call their son. Esmé would love to understand what they're saying, but they speak quickly. She catches phrases and individual words and observes that her daughter's face, so fresh and relaxed, is gradually changing to a sad, pained expression, one that isn't totally unfamiliar, however. Natalia needs something, *job*, she hears, *standing*, and then *legs,* and Naty shows Mrs. Dobbs a minuscule bluish mark on her calf, something that in thirty years might become a varicose vein. The dark-skinned woman shakes her head in a gesture of understanding and fright: it can't be, it can't be, she speaks rapidly to her husband in a conversation that grows louder, the two of them excuse themselves and get up to continue the conversation in private, they shut themselves in the kitchen for a very brief moment, Mr. Dobbs emerges with an even redder face than before, very disagreeably he holds out a check to Natalia, who looks at him with an expression of such genuine affection, with that wonderful smile, that crystal-clear gaze, which somehow manages to erase his furrowed brow, and immediately afterward, as if she can't contain herself, as if she feels an uncontrollable, slightly childish, impulse, the kind of passionate reaction North Americans attribute to Latinos, to Hispanics, as they're sometimes called, as if it's totally inevitable, she throws herself on the couple and embraces them, one by one, a tender, oh-so-sweet, grateful embrace for Mrs. Dobbs and another for Mr. Dobbs, maybe a little tighter for him, with a dangerous kiss, close to his mouth, unnoticed by Mrs. Dobbs, but not by Esmé, a kiss that the man accepts a little uncomfortably, but not without pleasure.

Esmeralda feels a strange, unexpected impulse. She would like to do something for them, for that couple who suffers and waits. She would like to defend them, protect them, warn them, but it's impossible: they would do anything to have their baby; they're committed, lost, totally at the mercy of the womb that's holding their son hostage.

JOURNAL ENTRY 24

I don't need to explain where the information about the airplane trip came from. On the other hand, it might interest the reader to know that I spent two months at the University of Virginia, teaching a Creative Writing class. It was a fascinating experience to work with students who were learning Spanish. At first, the fractured Spanish in which they wrote their responses to my assignments filled me with dread. I had a few Latino students in my class, and I sighed with relief whenever I reviewed one of their essays, written in correct Spanish. Little by little I realized that there were students who didn't have a command of the language, yet what they wrote was much richer, deeper, inventive, disturbing, and much more interesting than the texts of some of the native speakers. But isn't literature pure language? What is literature, where is it, that mystery which appears above and below the command of a language? Meanwhile, in this chapter, some concrete, arbitrary facts about the university, which don't have any function in the development of the plot, emphasize the plausibility of the story.

In an earlier version, Natalia turned twenty-one, legally coming of age. But I decided that it didn't suit my purposes to assign a precise date to the episode. By remaining ageless, Naty might be a little older, in her twenties, and I prefer it that way: at this point it's important that her actions and decisions not be mere adolescent blunders.

It's very difficult for me to finish this novel. I ask myself – without any possible answer – why I chose such a cruel theme. Of all the elements that come into play in constructing a literary text, the theme is the most mysterious, the most independent of the author's deliberate will. In his *Philosophy of Composition*, Edgar Allan Poe describes with strict rationality all the factors that led him to the composition of his poem "The Raven." There is no romantic swooning; all mysteries are unveiled, technique and craftsmanship are discussed, and "inspiration" is omitted entirely. Poe's quasi-scientific discourse falls short on just one point: when he tries to explain selection of a theme. Since it's a question of poetry, the theme should be beautiful, the author says, and what is more beautiful than the death of a lovely young woman? This is the same personal, arbitrary, ridiculous, inexplicable idea that each one of us has of beauty and of themes …

I'd like to be able to trick my readers by concealing from them how much is left till the end, but it's impossible. My readers have the book in their hand and can tell simply by looking that they have very few pages left to read, or a small percentage, if they're reading an e-book. The author, for her part, isn't unaware of this: she knows that the readers have concrete facts that anticipate a conclusion soon. To what extent does that physical certainty affect or direct the writing?

THE VISIT

Esmé is unsurprised when the voice on the telephone introduces itself as a friend of Natalia's. She's been waiting many days, many weeks for this: the voice, the call, the information. It's no surprise, but she's happy. It's very unusual for Natalia to be out of touch for such a long time. Now she's an adult woman, and she takes care of Esmé; she even protects her in many ways. There have been other occasions when Natalia didn't answer emails or messages for a certain amount of time or was unreachable on any of many cell phones, but somehow she always manages to communicate with Esmé to calm her down, more than once through a third person, like this time.

The man is nearby, he says, and he wants to drop in, to speak to her face to face. There's no reason to second-guess him. Esmé casts a dissatisfied, ill-humored glance around: she wants the messenger to form the best possible impression of Natalia's mother, but there's not much she can do at this point. She doesn't want to delay the meeting even one minute more than necessary. She decides that a quick clean-up will suffice, dusting off the table and gathering the newspapers, those paper journals that so many people have already given up, but which she still permits herself, like a small luxury.

The man is downstairs, ringing the buzzer on the intercom. His presence gives her hope after so many days of anguish and silence. Esmé takes a look at herself in the bathroom mirror and passes a brush quickly through her mussed hair, but doesn't apply makeup or perfume. Natalia's friend has a youthful voice, and meeting with a relatively young man always disturbs her: she's over sixty, and the loss of her youth, the loss of her sexual attractiveness, that powerful weapon, makes her feel unprotected, helpless, exposed. She especially takes infinite pains to ensure that the man (this one or any other) will not suspect any attempt at seduction on her part. Like a reverse paranoia, more than anything she fears making the other person feel pursued; she fears being perceived by others as an elderly stalker. That doesn't mean she's necessarily given up all possibilities, all such meetings: she still sees old male friends and is even open to forming new relationships, but she prefers men her own age or a little older. She feels she needs to be cautious now, desperately cautious.

He can't be more than forty or forty-five, the man who's walking into her house now, and nothing about him is especially noteworthy. Esmé is glad she doesn't have to describe him because she couldn't find the words to define his features. He's neither attractive nor especially ugly, a face like any other, hazel eyes, brown hair threaded with gray; he's wearing a pair of classic jeans, a dark green sweater on top of a white shirt. His style is neutral, perhaps overly neutral, and at first he strikes her as a little fatuous, but later he doesn't: then his expression starts to betray him. Yes, yes, he replies – with little conviction – to Esmé's first, anxious question: Yes, of course Natalia is fine, but he doesn't elaborate or offer too many details, nor does he articulate any message.

In a few minutes Esmeralda realizes that he's lied to her, that the man is no friend of her daughter's, that their futile, slightly random, conversation will offer her no information, no facts, nothing of what she's waiting for. On the contrary, the conversation, filled with more questions than answers, is intended to determine how much she knows about Natalia's activities.

And how much does she know, how much does she, Esmé, Natalia's mother, know about her daughter's activities? Nothing, or less than nothing. She hardly sees her. She knows that her daughter is a businesswoman, very successful, of course, on the board of directors of an Austrian laboratory with an unpronounceable name and excellent references on the Internet, a firm which her daughter refers to with a certain amount of respect, though never pronouncing it by name: the Laboratory, she says, with an obvious capital L. Esmé boasts a little, the minimum, indispensable amount, to her friends, correcting them when they speak of her daughter as a high ranking executive. No, not an executive, a director, she explains, insists: a partner, one of the owners. But that's not something she wants or needs to discuss with this man, who flashes a charming smile when she mentions the Austrian laboratory whose name he apparently knows quite well and is even able to pronounce, a famous laboratory with an impeccable history, and is the lady sure that it's there, in that laboratory and no other, that her daughter works? Yes, or course, Esmé is sure, completely sure, and even if she weren't, he'd never know; she has no reason to reveal her doubts to some stranger.

Natalia is very capable, very brilliant; it doesn't surprise her mother that she directs her firm's marketing department. Ever since she was a little girl she's had that ability, that vocation, that aptitude for earning money. She could have been a great economist if she had wanted to study, but she was impatient; from a very early age she chose to go directly into the business world, a good and successful daughter, always ready to help her out with money, although Esmé would rather not say too much about that, proud as she is of her own personal independence. She was the first of her friends to become emancipated from her parents, she managed to survive a separation without reducing her living space, and she was also successful in her own way, an advertising star, Esmé, although these days it's so hard for her to find free-lance jobs and she has to eke out a living by teaching business writing courses at a private university, and it embarrasses her more than she can say to accept money from her daughter for the past few years, even though Naty tries in every possible way to make her feel she's earning it, something that she doesn't even mention in front of the man, God knows why she hasn't thrown him out of her house yet, maybe because she prefers to handle this matter calmly, discreetly, maybe because the man is talking to her now, no doubt to distract her from her own mother, from Alcira, whom his friend Natalia, he assures her (but Esmé no longer believes a word he's saying) mentions so often.

Esmé has to admit (the exchange of words with the man is so formal, so conventional, that it allows her mind to wander effortlessly), she has to admit, but only to herself, that since her mother's death she's been feeling surprisingly alone, off-kilter. Only since then has she understood to what extent she had lived to rebel, to systematically, essentially oppose anything her mother suggested or said, and that now, without Alcira's cutting observations about everything in this world, Esmé simply doesn't know what to think.

But what does she know, how much does Esmé really know, about her daughter's activities? More than she'd like, less than she imagines. Natalia has an apartment in Buenos Aires, which she insisted on putting in her mother's name (It's so much easier that way, Mamá – you're the one who's always here, and you'll have to do paperwork for me from time to time), a spacious, four-room apartment in Puerto Madero, very comfortable for a single person who doesn't spend much time in the city in any case. It's a pleasure to see Naty when she comes back from one of her business trips, always traveling first class. It would have thrilled her grandmother, who placed so much importance on dressing well, to see her style, Esmé thinks: designer clothes, Ferragamo shoes, Bulgari jewelry, dresses and suits from Marc Jacobs, Kenzo, Armani, Vuitton luggage, all the bells and whistles of great prosperity. Sometimes she arrives accompanied, and Esmé welcomes each of her boyfriends, Argentine or foreign (everyone's called a boyfriend these days, she sometimes thinks, sighing), with the same enthusiasm, with the idea that the experience will be repeated, but none of them ever comes back. Natalia seems uninterested in making commitments. One thing's for sure: Esmé would never have told her mother that Naty carried a gun in her pretty Michael Kors handbag, remarkable now that Chanel is coming back into style. Alcira was of a different generation; she wouldn't have understood what insecurity is like these days, the danger of entering a house at night, a woman alone, the need to defend oneself from crime. Of course, she doesn't mention any of this (nor would she ever) to the man who has taken a seat, very comfortable, very relaxed, in one of the armchairs, without being invited, and who has refused coffee, but instead accepts a cup of tea, which he sips enthusiastically as he eats the chocolate-covered orange peel. More than once Natalia had explained the problems and dangers of industrial spying to Esmé, emphasizing the importance of not talking about her to strangers, of not giving out unnecessary information about her activities or trips.

Esmé doesn't want to do anything abrupt, nothing that would draw his attention. She pretends to accept his lie, to believe that he's a good friend of her daughter's, and the man stays for over an hour, talking of many things, remarking on the weather, the furniture, the Alonso reproduction that Esmé has placed above the loveseat. He's a pleasant person, not an ignoramus; he understands something about painting and painters; he knows the best place in Buenos Aires to find chocolate-covered orange peel, what a coincidence – they're *his* favorites, too – a little candy shop near El Ateneo bookstore. And he keeps dropping questions, absently, almost foolishly, to which Esmé keeps providing answers, just as absently, almost foolishly, evading, with a slickness that makes her feel proud, those few facts she possesses about her daughter's activities. For example, she knows, but will not say, that in addition to the apartment,

Naty has made many investments in the country, though for tax reasons, as she explained, she prefers to keep them in the name of corporations, something Esmé understands perfectly, because taxes have become all-consuming, relentless. How did the country manage in those bygone days of her childhood, her adolescence, when only businesses paid taxes, because the State didn't even try to collect taxes from individuals, and yet Argentina was so much wealthier, the middle-class was so much bigger, it was so much closer to being that famous and infamous breadbasket of the world that her parents and teachers had talked about? Naturally, she doesn't mention her daughter's investments to the man and slickly diverts the conversation when he touches on that subject. If the mysterious gentleman has come to investigate Natalia's property situation, she won't be the one to give him information.

Neither will she discuss that time when the Laboratory had problems with a regular account and Natalia had asked her to store some boxes she had received in the house. They were big boxes, unusually light, whose content Esmé peeked at just once, only to discover that they were filled with lots of smaller boxes, so reassuringly formal, well-marked with the logo of a brand she didn't recognize; and what luck that the boxes weren't in her house at the moment – they took up so much space, and it was impossible to cover them up or hide them. She imagined the man would be interested in seeing them, and what for. After all, it never happened again, and besides, she was sure, it had only been one of Natalia's silly ideas to make her feel better, so that Esmé could receive, without awkwardness, money that didn't come from her own pocket, as Natalia reassured her, but rather from the Laboratory. It was just that the paperwork could be so complicated sometimes that they preferred to give her the money in the form of a travel allowance, so that she could use it according to the needs of the moment.

Only for that reason, because she knew the money didn't come from Natalia's pocket, did Esmé accept – more than once – her daughter's paying her the equivalent of a luxury room in a five-star hotel for providing a room in her house to some foreigner who worked for the Laboratory and needed temporary lodging in the city. And what five-star hotel would be as comfortable as at your house? Naty woud say. The first time it was a surprise. The man's name (allegedly) was Antonio, and he showed up with Natalia, who introduced him as one of the firm's chauffeurs.

Antonio was a big, hefty guy, dressed in threadbare clothing that was too small on him and looked borrowed or like a hand-me-down. He spoke with a Latin American accent that Esmeralda couldn't recognize, and he acted very respectful and grateful. He stayed for three days, during which he didn't leave the apartment, ensconced in Naty's former room, listening on his cell phone all day long to something he finally made Esmé listen to, as well: Peruvian pop music, a sort of terribly sad Andean *cumbia*, melancholy tunes about doomed love.

"Do you work with my daughter?" Esmé asked at the first lunch they shared. She had prepared simple food for him: a roast with potatoes and onions, which the man praised and wolfed down voraciously.

"I was her chauffeur in Lima," the man said, blowing his nose in a rather dirty handkerchief, a kind Esmé had thought no longer existed. "Your daughter is a big shot, a real *grosa*," he added, using a very Argentine expression.

And it was useless to try to prolong the conversation on the subject of work, because Antonio only replied with a closed-mouth smile, for which he had very good reason: one of his front teeth was missing.

The Laboratory's employees, men and women, who stayed at Esmé's house for a very short time (never more than two or three days) were silent people. They hardly ever went out and spent a good portion of their stay closed up in the room.

Occasionally, very occasionally, Esmé tried to have a serious talk with Natalia. Her daughter would fix a honey-colored gaze on her and smile in the charming way her mother recognized from her childhood, that limpid, innocent smile, which was certainly not missing any teeth, and which transformed her into a surface as hard and impenetrable as a wall.

There was one time, only one, and of course Esmé wasn't about to discuss it, especially not that episode, with the man, who is now munching on chocolate-covered orange peel, and who, although he still hasn't said so, is showing his colors as a policeman, a police detective, more and more. One afternoon, during one of her daughter's rare visits, they were watching TV together. Natalia had put on comfortable clothing, a jogging suit, clothes for drinking *mate*, she called them. They were watching, not paying much attention. Esmé held the remote, skipping over the sports programs, kids' shows, a couple of cable channels, a few cooking shows, a little bit about sharks, some reality TV, a few torture scenes (practically every other channel had a scene where a tied-up, half-naked person was groaning through a gag; Esmé passed over these rapidly, returning again and again to the sharks, so relaxing despite the narrator's ominous voice), until she found a news channel. Leave that on, Natalia had said, and "that" was the story of a murder, the killing of three young men at a shopping mall, which the announcer described as a vendetta, something that vaguely had to do with the pharmaceutical industry and cocaine manufacturing. They mentioned the word "precursors," a term that no longer meant people whose talent or good will turned them into visionaries, ahead of their time, as in the good old days; now the word "precursor" had taken on a dangerous, harmful, criminal connotation: the journalists spoke gravely about the precursors of cocaine production as if they knew exactly what it was all about. And for one instant, only one instant, Emsé dropped the screen of naïveté with which she had always covered up her convictions; for one instant she stopped playing the fool, not just before her friends, but to herself, before her own conscience, and in an impulse, regretting her words as soon as she had uttered them, she asked Natalia:

"Did you people have something to do with that?"

And incredibly, Natalia, allowing herself for an instant, but only for an instant, to enter that breach that was opening in the fog that usually dominated their relationship, their conversations, replied in the same simple, direct tone:

"No. The Laboratory doesn't deal with that. I once told you that cocaine wasn't my thing. I was young, I was foolish, and I didn't understand anything. But I wasn't mistaken about that."

And so ended that short, but clear, conversation to which they never returned and which Esmé would never disclose to the man who was now putting his alibi, his disguise, aside, who was introducing himself formally before leaving, revealing his obvious identity, standing up, saying horrible words to Esmé, words she has no reason to believe.

"We know that you've had no news of your daughter for a long time, Señora Esmeralda. The news we have isn't good. We believe that it happened shortly after her last visit to the country, that it was a confrontation between gangs, and that her body was thrown into the sea, possibly from a small plane."

The man leaves. Esmé closes the door gently, but with a gesture that makes it clear that she's closing it forever, and her mind beings to spin crazily, feverishly, around his words. It's a lie, of course it's a lie. It was his last attempt to get her to talk, to drag information out of her. It's obvious that the guy knows the family history. They know perfectly well what happened with Regina: that story about Natalia and the death flight seems like an intelligent lie, well crafted, perfect for destabilizing a person who has suffered what Esmé suffered during the dictatorship. But he didn't succeed. Esmé remained firm, quiet, she didn't cry. She even said goodbye to the man elegantly, like a lady. Her mother would have been proud: like a lady.

Alone at last, sitting in the green corduroy armchair,

the most comfortable one, the one with the clear imprint of her head on the headrest, the corduroy squashed by its light weight, the reading chair, the one that contains and embraces her without asking anything in return, without demanding anything, without asking anything; the chair is almost like her mother, how she would have loved for it to be her mother. Esmeralda allows herself to try to understand what she's feeling, this strange sensation that presses on her chest but won't let her cry. And she wonders. She wonders – as she's wondered so many times before, as on those many sleepless nights when her thoughts rambled along in every possible direction, along every road – about the central question of her life. She wonders how and why and in what way it was her participation, her responsibility, her monstrous fault, but especially when, when, when it all began. Ever since she stopped smoking, Esmé has had a recurring dream: In her dream she suddenly finds herself smoking a cigarette and she knows she's fallen again, she knows that she's trapped in an addiction again, and that this time it's forever, that she'll never be able to get free, but in the dream she can't seem to remember the first time, the precise moment, now erased from her mind, when she lit the first cigarette again, the fatal, lethal one, the one that has led her back to smoking like before, as always. And so, without any possible answer, her mind now skips untidily, backward and forward, over the story of her maternity, the story of her life, trying to find the starting point, the key moment when the error, the horror, was unleashed. And she can't even cry.

She ought to call Guido to tell him about the detective's visit, about his terrible parting words. Maybe he'll decide to come for a few days, she thinks; maybe he'll come to be with her; maybe he, too, will have a need to talk and be together and remember without words, because sometimes words are useless, stupid, heavy as blowflies. No doubt Guido will want to embrace her, just as she needs to embrace him at this moment, not because she still loves him, but because no one else in the world loved (loves?) Natalia as he does, as she does. While she resolves to phone Guido, Esmé clings to the armrests of the green chair, leaning on them so she can stand. She stumbles toward the kitchen, unthinkingly, carrying out the series of mechanical, automatic, stereotypical gestures necessary to make herself a cup of tea. She looks with hatred at the tea kettle on the fire, the water that keeps boiling, turning into steam as soon as it reaches 212 degrees, as if everything were the same, as if nothing in the universe had changed. On her chest, restricting her breathing, drying out the source of her tears, is that strange sensation that overcomes the pain, the horror, the guilt, the sadness, that sensation that she is still incapable of recognizing, of accepting.

But she's not dead, Esmé says to herself. Natalia isn't dead. She's only *missing*, only, only, and that only isn't enough for her. What's enough is the near certainty of Natalia's phony friend, whom she keeps thinking of as "the man." What's enough is the word missing, which in Argentina sounds like death. She can't stop thinking about Regina, her sister, her perfect corpse, so carefully restored by the funeral home, which managed to conceal her wounds so artfully, the corpse that they nonetheless decided to leave in a closed casket to avoid the inevitable, cruel curiosity of relatives and friends. In the days when militants disappeared, leaving their loved ones with the torture of doubt, they had been granted the privilege of having a corpse to honor, to take leave of, to remember. While now, when people's disappearances have been reduced to runaway teenagers, kidnappings, sexual slavery, no less serious or terrible for their relatives, but definitely reduced to smaller, less frequent statistics, now her daughter Natalia has disappeared. What does Esmé feel? What does she feel like a brick in the middle of her chest, pressing down, restricting her heartbeat? What is that thing that keeps her from crying, that thing that moves to the forefront and becomes entwined with love and pain and horror?

Then, suddenly, she understands. She realizes what she's feeling, and the understanding falls upon her like the vortex of a breaking wave that drags her, scraping her skin against the sandy ocean floor, then submerges and suffocates her and makes her doubt, but only for a moment, that her lungs once were able to inhale and exhale air.

What she feels is relief, a great relief that her daughter isn't there, and a terrible, terrible fear that she'll return. Only now do love, pain, and horror fill her chest and Esmé, at last, can cry.

Ana María Shua

Ana María Shua was born in Buenos Aires in 1951. At the age of 15, she won her first literary contest, resulting in the publication of her first work, a book of poems titled *El sol y yo (The Sun and I)*. Since that auspicious beginning, she has published more than thirty books.

Shua was graduated from the Universidad Nacional de Buenos Aires with a degree in pedagogy, although she has never practiced that profession. She has, however, worked as a publicist, journalist, and screenwriter.

In 1980, her novel, *Soy paciente (Patient)*, was awarded the Losada Prize. Her other novels include: *Los amores de Laurita (The Loves of Laurita)*, converted into a motion picture; *El libro de los recuerdos (The Book of Memory)* for which she received a Guggenheim Fellowship; and *La muerte como efecto secundario (Death as a Side Effect)*, which received the Primer Premio Municipal of Buenos Aires. Shua is also recognized as one of the principal Latin American cultivators of the *microrrelato*, a genre of extremely short fiction, exemplified by such collections as: *La sueñera, Casa de Geishas* and *Botánica del caos*. In 2016 she earned the Juan José Arreola Prize for minifiction. Her novel *El peso de la tentación (The Weight of Temptation)*, was published by Emecé in Argentina and in English translation by Andrea G. Labinger (University of Nebraska Press). *Hija* (*Daughter*) was published by Emecé (2016).

Ana María Shua's work has been widely anthologized, translated, and published in Italy, Germany, Serbia, Korea, and China. *Hija* was published in Arabic in Kuwait.

Shua resides in Buenos Aires with her husband and three daughters.

Andrea G. Labinger

Andrea G. Labinger specializes in translating Latin American prose fiction. Among the many authors she has translated are Sabina Berman, Carlos Cerda, Mempo Giardinelli, Ana María Shua, Alicia Steimberg, and Luisa Valenzuela.

Call Me Magdalena, Labinger's translation of Steimberg's *Cuando digo Magdalena* (University of Nebraska Press, 2001) received Honorable Mention in the PEN International-California competition. *The Rainforest*, her translation of Steimberg's *La selva*, and *Casablanca and Other Stories*, an anthology of Edgar Brau's short stories, translated in collaboration with Donald and Joanne Yates, were both finalists in the PEN-USA competition for 2007. *The Island of Eternal Love*, her translation of Cuban novelist Daína Chaviano's *La isla de los amores infinitos*, was published by Riverhead/Penguin in 2008.

Other novel-length translations include: *The Confidantes*, a translation of Angelina Muñiz-Huberman's *Las confidentes* (Gaon Books, 2009); *Death as a Side Effect*, a translation of Ana María Shua's *La muerte como efecto secundario* (University of Nebraska Press, 2010); *Friends of Mine*, a translation of Ángela Pradelli' *Amigas mías* (Latin American Literary Review Press, 2012); and *The End of the Story*, a translation of Liliana Heker's *El fin de la historia*

(Biblioasis, 2012); *The Weight of Temptation* (*El peso de la tentación*) by Ana María Shua (Nebraska, 2012) and *Borges and Mathematics* (*Borges y la matemática*) by Guillermo Martínez (Purdue, Fall 2012).

In 2013 *World Literature Today* listed *The End of the Story* among the "75 notable translations of the year."

Labinger's translation of Gustavo Gac-Artigas' novel, *And All of Us Were Actors: A Century of Light and Shadow* (*Y todos* éramos *actores . . . en un siglo de luz y sombra,* Ed. Nuevo Espacio, 2017) won second prize at the International Latino Book Awards Ceremony, California State University, 2018.

Gesell Dome, Labinger's translation of Guillermo Saccomanno's *Cámara Gesell,* was awarded a 2014 PEN/HeimTranslation Fund grant and was published by Open Letter Books in 2016. It was also a finalist for the Firecracker Award, sponsored by the Community of Literary Magazines and Presses. Another of her Saccomanno novel translations, *77* (Open Letter 2019) was featured in *The New York Times* "Globetrotting"section (Feb. 2019) and designated by *Vanity Fair* magazine as one of "the six must-read books from around the world"(Feb. 2019). Most recently, her translation of *77* was a finalist for the Best Translated Book Awards.